CRAFTING THE WORD

Untitled
Kundo Yumnam

CRAFTING THE WORD

Writings from Manipur

Edited by

THINGNAM ANJULIKA SAMOM

zubaan

ZUBAAN
128 B Shahpur Jat, 1st Floor
New Delhi 110 049
Email: contact@zubaanbooks.com
Website: www.zubaanbooks.com

First published by Zubaan Publishers Pvt. Ltd 2019

Published in association with the Sasakawa Peace Foundation

✒ THE SASAKAWA PEACE FOUNDATION

10 9 8 7 6 5 4 3 2 1

ISBN 978 93 85932 80 9

Zubaan is an independent feminist publishing house based in New
Delhi with a strong academic and general list. It was set up as an
imprint of India's first feminist publishing house, Kali for Women,
and carries forward Kali's tradition of publishing world-quality
books to high editorial and production standards. *Zubaan* means
tongue, voice, language, speech in Hindustani. Zubaan publishes
in the areas of the humanities, social sciences, as well as in fiction,
general non-fiction, and books for children and young adults under
its Young Zubaan imprint.

Typeset in Baskerville 11/13 by Jojy Philip
Printed and bound at Replika Press Pvt. Ltd., India

Contents

CONTENTS

Acknowledgements

A collection of women's writings that not only reflects the richness of Manipuri literature, but also fuses the idea of gender equality with women's quest for self-identity has been a long-awaited project. I am thankful for the opportunity to compile and edit such a collection in *Crafting the Word: Writings from Manipur*.

I would like to thank Urvashi Butalia for this opportunity to showcase women's writings from Manipur, Zubaan for publishing this anthology, the Sasakawa Peace Foundation for making this possible with their sponsorship, and all the wonderful women of Leimarol Khorjeikol (Leikol) for their rich creativity and enthusiasm. I would also like to thank Kundo Yumnam for her wonderful artworks, and the team of translators who were fearless in their translations and patient during the excruciating editing process.

We present *Crafting the Word: Writings from Manipur* with the hope that this compilation will be a precursor to many more such publications in the future.

Introduction

THINGNAM ANJULIKA SAMOM

A casual flip through tourism brochures and state government calendars brings up some stock images of Manipuri women – as coy dancing girls, or as haggling vendors in the renowned women's market, the Nupi Keithel, or as the stone-encased figures of the women warriors of the Nupi Lan (the Women's War of 1904 and 1939) grappling with gun-wielding soldiers. Images of softness blend seamlessly with the strength and responsibility that seems to define the identity of the Manipuri woman.

Yet, apart from this identity bestowed by society and nation, who really is the Manipuri woman? Where does she stand? What are her beliefs, thoughts and views? How do Manipuri women see themselves? Are they the forbearing, accommodating, enduring, courageous and self-sacrificing spirits that they have been typecast as over the centuries? Or are they just beautiful and ornamental beings resigned to a wallflower-like existence under patriarchy? Are they also agents of change and protest – as exemplified by the Meira

Paibi women and their night-long vigils to shield their sons from army atrocities, the Naga women praying and marching together for peace, or the Iron Woman of Manipur, Irom Sharmila Chanu, who went on the world's longest hunger strike of 16 years to demand the repeal of a draconian law that tramples all human rights?

Over the last few years, the women of Manipur have been repeatedly studied, analysed and reviewed. Many pages and books have been devoted to them, and much has been written about them. In this book, for the first time 27 women from Manipur – a visual artist and 26 writers – come together to give us their idea of who the Manipuri woman is, to share their experiences of being a woman in a patriarchal order, and to tell us about the conditions, trials, tribulations and jubilations of their lives. This group of writers, who include four Sahitya Akademi winners – Maharaj Kumari Binodini, Sunita Ningombam, Arambam Ongbi Memchoubi and Moirangthem Borkanya – write primarily in Meiteilon (Manipuri), Tangkhul and English. Together they have produced some of the best literature in Manipur.

Our selection features women writers across different time periods, literary styles, genres, ethnic communities and languages – each delineating the woman that they see around them and the woman that they feel they ought to be. The stories, poems, essays and the graphic story in this collection speak of the women of Manipur – their experiences, their loves and desires, their suppression in a patriarchal society, their negotiations and compromises with society and tradition, their struggles to grow and forge a new path, and their emergence from suppressive shells like butterflies spreading their colourful wings.

Maharaj Kumari Binodini, the first Manipuri woman to pen a short story and also the first Sahitya Akademi awardee among Manipuri woman writers, sensitively portrays her own experience as a student at Shantiniketan and the bond of love she shared with her friends in her personal essay, 'Girls' Hostel'. The weaving of little details drawn from her experiences and her environment, the simplicity of style and narration that belies her acute observation of life around her, and the sensitive portrayal of the human heart that marks the beauty of Binodini's writing, is clearly reflected in this story. What is also significant is that she studied at Shantiniketan as an international student, as a princess from the erstwhile independent kingdom of Manipur. In 'Girls' Hostel' she says,

> Once Sarojini Naidu came to our convocation at Vishva-Bharati. There was a huge reception. Word came to Sri Bhavana: Send some girls to give flowers to Sarojini, and include that Manipuri girl too. She must wear her national dress, and so on. They must have liked our phaneks a great deal.

From this exploration of self-identity and experience arises the question, where is a woman's place in the patriarchal order? What are her rights? How has she been treated and viewed? Sanjembam Bhanumati, normally a traditionalist in her writings, raises an age-old issue that has long dogged girl children across communities in her poem, 'Where Is A Daughter's Home?', where she charts the journey of a girl child from childhood to marriage and death, and her place in her immediate family and society.

Where is a daughter's home?
Where is my true homestead?
Will I leave without knowing it?
Depart thus, baffled and lost?
('Kadaidano Ningol Iyumbo': *Aroiba Wahang*, 2001)

Is this a recent phenomenon or has it been in existence for centuries? In her signature satirical style, Ningombam Sanatombi examines the lives and experiences of important goddesses of Hindu mythology in her short story, 'Sati Interview', and comes to the conclusion that women have been oppressed, suppressed and denied their rights from time immemorial.

One would assume from the many references, historical incidents and greater visibility on the socio-political and economic front, that Manipuri women have a higher social standing in the gender order. However, this deification of women is not even skin deep and instances of gender equality are the exception rather than the rule. As Ningombam Surma shows us in her short story, 'The Defeat', despite so much talk about gender equality, the male patriarch is not ready to really accept the idea that women are able to stand on their own. He is unwilling to have a woman identified by her own work or to stand behind a woman himself.

This is the hypocrisy that has characterised patriarchal society for long, and oppressive rules of acceptable behaviour have taken deep roots in communities.

For the older generation of women writers, it was a tough task to totally break free from this predicament. Having been conditioned by the patriarchal process, they became

traditionalists and purists themselves. Lairenlakpam Ibemhal
speaks of this beautifully in her poem, 'The Noose'.

> To my mother
> By my grandmother
> To my grandmother
> By my great-grandmother
> To my great-grandmother
> By my great- great-grandmother
> She too
> By the one who birthed her
> One after another
> Through the buried
> Many centuries
> Entrusted
> This *huigang*
> This dog-leash
> Like a newlywed's necklace
> On my neck
> Calmly garlanding
> My
> Dear Mother
> Said –
> 'This is your adornment!'
>
> ('Konggoi': *Nongthanggi Innaphi*, 2002)

It takes a mighty leap of faith for women at large and
women writers too to de-condition themselves, to question and
challenge the status quo. And yet they do break free, emerge
slowly and steadily, step by small step, in little acts of defiance,
to partake in the creation of a new world order where women
can do what they want, and be who they wish to be.

But
I disliked it
Could never agree to it
Because
I saw
Through the forcible misinterpretation
Of the significance of this ornament
How you all
To those many
Named them
As you wished, and
Dragged them
In whichever directions you choose
Like a loyal dog
Or
Like obedient bullocks yoked to a cart
Therefore
I've cut off thus today
That which you all have forcibly
Made into a murderous rope
This noose around my neck.

('Konggoi': *Nongthanggi Innaphi*, 2002)

Kundo Yumnam's 'A Market Story' is a beautiful and thought-provoking graphic story that presents the frequent confrontation between these little acts of rebellion by the newer generation and an older order of deeply conditioned women who expect them to carry forth the patriarchal order – whether in dress, food habits or familial responsibilities.

The selection in this volume constitutes those little acts of defiance, of protest, of challenge, and the reawakening of a woman's free soul. For instance, these women writers, across ages, start questioning the concepts of traditional morality and purity which are often used to discriminate against and oppress women, as also the notion of women being the upholders of morality and forming the identity of their society.

In her poem, 'Woman', Koijam Santibala presents the quintessential problem that women face – their deification as goddesses on the one hand, and their branding as being wanton for expressing themselves, on the other. Chongtham Subadani feels that even the much decorated and loved dancing girls, the *apsaras* in Indra's court, have started rebelling at the denial of their rights in her poem, 'When the Apsaras Awakened'.

Kshetrimayum Subadani questions the existing concepts of morality laid down by male-dominated society in her short story, 'As Spring Arrives'. Is it just or right to have different sets of moral values for men and women? Who should judge whom? These are the questions that she poses through her protagonist Ibemnungshi, who is driven out of her home by her promiscuous and oppressive husband on false accusations of having had illicit relations with another man. Subadani also questions a society that creates certain 'norms' and is willing to go to any lengths to impose them.

Dr Chongtham Jamini, being an educator by profession, has been engaged in questioning the stereotypes and prejudices that work against women in Manipuri society. In her short story, 'Kitchen Duty', she questions the concepts of domestic responsibility and purity in a patriarchal society. Ibochouba is designated to cook the meal for the day as tradition does not allow a menstruating woman to enter the kitchen or cook, and in the process he learns that significant work is involved in carrying out his wife's household chores which he had previously dismissed as being insignificant.

Ayung Tampakleima Raikhan's poem, 'Adornments', too, rejects the hypocrisy that accompanies patriarchal notions of morality and purity that are intended to make women subjugate themselves to men.

> I touched your feet one day, in front of all
> Tonight at this silent hour you suck my toes
> Say whose feet are pure? Whose impure?
> And what is purity, do let us hear?
>
> ('Leiteng': *Samjirei*, 2010)

Does a woman have the right to choose? Is she able to stand alone, independent and firm? Through little rebellions and their rejection of the concept that a woman should always be under the protective care of a man, the writers assert the independent spirit of women. Bimabati Thiyam Ongbi's short story, 'The Detour' is a touching sketch depicting the meeting of former lovers in the unlikeliest place and situation, and the nostalgic tug-of-war of emotions that follows. Yet, the young widow stands firm in her decision to struggle alone without leaning on others for support, no matter how tempting and how convenient that may be. In Haobam Satyabati's short story, 'My Husband's Child', a widow seeks refuge for herself and her child in the socially accepted institution of marriage, but when her child is denied justice, she rejects the marriage and walks out.

Lairenlakpam Ibemhal calls for a review of gender roles through her poem, 'Shadow', wherein she presents a clever reversal of roles. Arambam Ongbi Memchoubi delves into local myths and legends to study the condition of women. She urges women to not confine themselves to domestic roles and child-rearing, and emphasies the need for women's political participation in order to create a new world.

> Come, come, O, Nonggoubi
> Today, the world will be created anew
> This journey is towards the light,
> Come, come, let's create together!
>
> ('Nonggoubi': *Nonggoubi*, 1984)

Memchoubi has portrayed the archetypal mother in her poem, 'My Beloved Mother', a woman who doggedly shoulders her responsibilities, and carries the burden of both the past and the future on her back.

> I peeped in, curious to know what's inside,
> Inside the basket, in Mother's basket, I saw
> Her old husband,
> Her youthful son.
> Bewildered, I asked,
> 'Why Mother, what is this?'
> Mother looked at me once,
> And said slowly –
> 'If I don't carry them, how will they survive?'
> Without any further words,
> She walked away, as before,
> Calmly, solemnly,
> My beloved Mother.
>
> ('Eigi Palem Nungshibi': *Eigi Palem
> Nungshibi*, 1998)

Moirangthem Borkanya reflects on the loss of individuality and self-image of women in her poem, 'This Storm'.

> In one fragment my eye
> in another my cheek
> Likewise legs, hands, chest, neck –
> everything is in pieces today
> these shadows on the pieces of the broken mirror.
>
> ('Nongleise': *Yenningtha Nangna Khongdoi*
> *Hullakpasida*, 2008)

While she expresses her anger at the cause of this distortion, the male patriarch, in sharp juxtaposition, continues to enjoy his freedom.

> Though for generations
> remained covered with a black veil,
> barred by mountains,
> an unstoppable storm churns today
> from thousands and thousands of hearts
> of the images reflected in the shards of the broken mirror.
> This rising storm is not in vain
> it does not blow any other way, except yours
> This tempest is aimed towards you
> only towards you.
>
> ('Nongleise': *Yenningtha Nangna Khongdoi*
> *Hullakpasida*, 2008)

Though women writers have spoken about gender relations, drawn attention to the imbalances that exist, questioned them, and even challenged them at times, there have been very few writings on a subject that is central to the idea of womanhood – women's sexuality, related biological factors, gender identity, sexual preferences, and so on – topics which patriarchal morality deems taboo. Neither have there been many explorations of non-binary gender identities and relationships.

In a rare instance, Ningombam Sunita writes about a woman's desire in her story, 'The Debt Repaid.' The young widow Lalita's daily light-hearted banter with the *paan* seller Shyamo take a deeper and more intimate turn when she unexpectedly finds herself sexually attracted to him. However, Lalita's exploration of her desire ends with her deciding to adhere to tradition. Though widow remarriage is not frowned upon in Manipuri society, Lalita is conflicted on this front. In the end, she chooses to stay away from Shyamo and continue her life with the memory of her dead husband's love.

In 'Nightmare', faced with the obstructive forces of conservative society, Leishna succumbs to her mother's wishes and meets up with a man. Her partner Somorani (Somo) commits suicide. It is as if both Sunita and Nee knew that conservative society has no place for a woman's desire or for a transman and his partner's 'happily ever after'. Nevertheless, both writers open the door for more forays into these topics.

The youngest generation in the selection are more at ease in their expression and choice of theme. Haobijam Chanu Prema is one of the young writers who stands out for her choice of theme, her descriptive narrative poetry and her tongue-in-cheek outbursts. She immerses us in a world of innocence contrasted with patriarchal society in her dramatic narrative on menstruation, 'Monthly Flower'. She not only portrays the concepts of purity, social taboos, gender biases, prejudices and superstitions linked with menstruation, but the beauty of her poem is also in the vivid narration of a young girl's first introduction to and experience with menstruation. With the choice of theme for this poem, she shatters the patriarchal shroud of silence that defines what can be said or not said about womanhood and/or women's experience, and thus makes the personal political.

> In the riverbed with my girlfriends
> Happiness overflowing
> Swimming, dipping, playing,
> When suddenly wanting to go for the big one,
> Head to toe, my whole body
> Fully drenched, I ran up
> And in our latrine
> Walled with hedge-plants
> While I squatted, listening to the radio drama
> You had
> Made my heart jump.
>
> Oh, Monthly Flower!
> Seeing you
> The hair on my scalp rose
> Ho, Mother! Is it a leech bite?
> Soaked in sweat
> How I shook in fright,
> I recall as if 'twas yesterday.
> ('Tha-gi Lei': *Punshi Khongchatsida*, 2011)

This fearless expression of feelings, unfettered by patriarchal or traditional norms, finds its place in English, an adopted language preferred by many of the younger group of writers – perhaps as a result of their education or long sojourns away from home, either for educational or professional purposes in other parts of the country, and even outside India.

Natalie Nk presents a feminist inquiry into the patriarchal notions of womanhood, and her reactions to it through the clever metaphor of skin in her poem, 'The Skin of Woman'.

> The skin of a woman must resemble hills:
> undulating, patient under the sheets. Sentient
> to a titillating touch. Lenient as the stem of a bud.
> It should be held up by satin and lace —
> for certain eyes only.
>
> Yet skin is skin, and the skin of a woman
> bears the scars of a knife,
> criss-crossing the top of the fingers.
> It carries the smell of potatoes and fish.
> It reeks of sweat, musky and thick,
> stains the satin and lace, falling from grace.
> ('The Skin of Woman': Unpublished, 2018)

Yuimi Vashum's poems are touching personal narratives of her own experience of child sexual abuse. Through her powerful use of words and images, she questions the silence that surrounds a discussion that ought to be the most important for all genders.

Hidden behind a piece of cloth,
They talked about it in hushed tones.
Why would mother(s) not talk about the vagina?
Don't they know it's as important as my limbs?
Why will they not tell me
To scream and sprint if someone tries to put their
hands in my
underwear?

('Breaking the Shame': *Love. Lust. And
Loyalty*, 2018)

The strength in Yuimi is endless, and she rises from her struggles, the ghosts and the haunting, like a phoenix, strong, fiery and powerful.

Lest my children grow Mute
Spineless
Submissive.
I spend it all
And refuse to be our mothers
Who accept injustice like a birthright.
…
Today, I speak
And reclaim the voice our mothers long buried.

('Here I am, After All These Years':
Love. Lust. And Loyalty, 2018)

The writings in this volume also touch upon the ongoing armed conflict in the state, reflecting on its impact on the lives of women. This comes through in Ningombam Satyabati's heart-rending sketch of a woman who loses her children and husband in a bomb blast in the short story, 'My Children's Photographs'; Maya Nepram's depiction of the common people's struggle for life amidst the conflict in the short story, 'Crimson Tides'; and Mufidun Nesha's portrayal of a mother waiting for her child in her poem, 'At the Morgue'.

> For the news
> Of her child taken forcibly away
> At gunpoint
> Now untraceable, without any clues
> Sitting at the morgue, awaits
> The poor mother.
>
> Of those taken away beyond the gate
> Of those concealed, disappeared,
> The destination is the morgue.
>
> ('Morgue Ta': *Mingshel da Leichil*, 2006)

Ghanapriya's short story, 'The Day That Dusked at Dawn' looks at another aspect of conflict – the agency of women as active participants in it, while RK Sanahanbi (Likkhombi) Chanu presents a bleak future wherein even unborn children are unwilling to be born for fear of the conflict and the chaos it brings to society.

Tonjam Sarojini's poem, 'Don't Wait' details the atrocities and oppressions carried out under the Armed Forces Special Powers Act (1958). Comparing the draconian law to a bloodthirsty tiger on a hunt, she urges it to go away. Sarojini's other poem, 'Torch Warriors' is about the struggles of the Meira Paibi women, who do not have fame or achievements as ends in their struggle. At the core of their work is the mother's instinct to protect her child.

No, it isn't to raise the victory flag
Atop Himalayan peaks
No, it isn't to raise cries of victory
In the battlefields of the world.

It's only because of the desire
To hold in their embrace
A living child of their own.

('Meira Lanmi': *Lan Khammu Ima*, 2006)

Last but not the least, Aruna Nahakpam's essay, 'The Journey of Women's Writing in Manipuri Literature' takes us on a tour of the progress of Manipuri literature with special reference to the emergence and development of women's writing. The essay discusses socio-political conditions and their impact on women's status so as to better chart women's writing in Manipur.

The stories, poems and essays in this compilation were selected through an intense process of discussion, review, analysis and self-learning with the active collaboration of and consultations with Manipur's all-women writers' literary group, 'Leimarol Khorjeikol', also popularly known as 'Leikol'. Though the project initially aimed at bringing together the works of just twenty women writers, the existence of a large number of women writers and the realisation of the immense productivity and fertile creativity of their works led us to incorporate twenty-six writers and a visual artist in this book. Even the task of shortlisting writers and their works became an extremely lengthy and difficult exercise due to the wealth of available material.

The selected works have been translated into English

by an energetic group of translators, all excelling in their respective profession as writers, poets, filmmakers, academics, creative artists and innovators. The translators – mostly first-timers, though some have done a few translations before – went through a workshop and mentoring process. After an initial draft translation, the translators and writers met in a translation workshop wherein they had an in-depth discussion on the texts again with the writers themselves in order to review their own analysis and understanding of the text and the translation. For many of the writers, this was a first time opportunity to be able to voice their concerns and views on the translation. At every point of the translation and editing process, both writers and translators were kept in the loop – making the whole process a very communicative and involved exercise.

What sets apart this venture is not only the fact that this is the first time that an anthology of writings by women writers from Manipur is to be published by a 'mainstream' and renowned publisher like Zubaan, but also the thematic approach to the book – the exploration of women's self and identity – along with the collaboration with an all-women literary body, Leikol. Therefore, this compilation itself has involved an active agency in women's quest for identity and equality.

The Journey of Women's Writing in Manipuri Literature

Nahakpam Aruna

Introduction

Manipuri women have held a special place in the cultural, traditional, social and economic history of the state. Yet, their domestic existence continues to be strictly governed by tradition and custom. Paradoxically, their social and political activism, pioneering social and economic ownership and, at times, their resistance to colonial imperialism, as evident in the two Nupi Lans[1] or Women's Wars, and in more recent history, the Meira Paibi[2] movement, are lauded all over the world.

---

[1] In 1904, they rose against the imperialistic British order commanding Manipuri men to bring teak wood from Kabaw Valley and rebuild the burnt house of a British officer. The second Nupi Lan in 1939 was an uprising of these women to stop the export of locally produced rice out of Manipur, which had created an artificial famine in the state. In both instances, they emerged victorious.

[2] The Meira Paibi (lit. 'torch-bearing women') movement of Manipur

In the field of literature, too, their contribution has been evident from the time when literary forms mainly existed in the oral tradition. Women have been significant contributors and reservoirs of folk tales such as *phunga wari* and lyrical forms such as *naoshum eshei*, *phoushu eshei*, *khullang eshei* and *khunung eshei*. The invocations and oracles of the shamanistic Maibis (women oracles) can also be regarded as a form of semi-literary narrative.

Though written texts are recorded to have existed as far back as the eighth century in Manipur, it was only in what is considered the modern period of Manipuri literature, that is, the second half of the twentieth century, that the women of Manipur began writing.

THE GROWTH OF MANIPURI LITERATURE

During the early period of Manipuri literature (extending from early history to the seventeenth century), literary works mostly existed in the form of royal chronicles, ritual songs, tales of heroism and allegories written in the archaic Meitei Mayek script by anonymous, unnamed male authors. Some of these texts are *Numit Kappa*, *Hijen Harao*, *Panthoibi Khonggul*, *Poireiton Khunthokpa* and *Cheitharon Kumbaba*. Among the tribal communities living in the hills, literature continued to exist as songs and folklore in the absence of a written script.

The socio-cultural, religious and literary history of Manipur witnessed a tremendous change when Hinduism replaced the native Sanamahi worship among the Meitei population in the valley. The Meitei king, Meidingu

---

is a women's social movement to protect human rights against the atrocities of the armed forces during counter-insurgency movements in the state.

Pamheiba (1690–1751) made Hinduism the official religion and ordered the mass burning of the old texts or *puyas* to sever any connection with the older way of life. Following this incident, known as *puya meithaba*, Bengali and Sanskrit began to play an important role in religious invocations, ritualistic songs and cultural performances like *Nat Sankirtana*, *Raas Leela*, *Goura Leela*, and so on. Translations of Hindu texts such as the *Ramayana*, the *Mahabharata* and the *Bhagavat Gita* were carried out on a wide scale. The entry and adoption of a new religion brought with it new societal, cultural and religious mores, including many which ascribed new roles and boundaries to women. Gender roles, ideals and stereotypes ascribed by the *Manusmriti*, as well as concepts like untouchability and Sati (widow immolation), which came to be widely popularised by the new elite group of religious converts, found reflection in the literary works of the time.

Manipur underwent another socio-political and cultural transition almost a century later with the Burmese occupation from 1819 to 1826. This was known as the Seven Years Devastation or *Chahi Taret Khuntakpa*, and it took place during the reign of Maharaja Marjit Singh. The Devastation not only led to the mass killing and exodus of the local populace, but also initiated alliances with the British Empire during the First Anglo-Burmese War. The Yandaboo Peace Treaty in 1826 facilitated the return of the Manipuri people to the kingdom and recognised Gambhir Singh as the king, but also established the office of a British political agent in Manipur by 1835.

It was, however, only in 1891 after the defeat of Manipur in the Anglo-Manipuri War that the kingdom came under British rule. The British occupation opened a new chapter in the socio-political and economic arenas of the land, heralding Westernisation in the form of newly-created roads, electricity, bicycles, western (formal) education, and so on, besides putting an end to existing oppressive systems such as forced labour (*lallup*), selling of women as servants and public humiliation in the markets as a punitive method. It also marked the beginning of the modern period of Manipuri literature.

Christianity gradually replaced indigenous worship in the hills through the efforts of missionaries such as Reverend William Pettigrew, who not only set up a number of schools, but also wrote many important books (*Meitei Primer, Basic Arithmetic, English-Bengali-Manipuri Dictionary, Manipuri (Meitei) Grammar with illustrative sentences, Tangkhul Naga Grammar and Dictionary (Ukhrul dialect) with illustrative sentences*. Pettigrew translated the New Testament into the Tangkhul dialect of Ukhrul (1926), romanising the script of the native language.

With the establishment of formal education in Manipur after the setting up of Johnstone Middle English School (for boys) in 1885, English and the vernacular language replaced Bengali or Sanskrit as the medium of instruction. Most textbooks were, however, translated or adapted from Bengali. The new Manipuri textbooks were also printed using the Bengali or Devanagari script, and Meitei Mayek was relegated to the use of only a handful of local scholars known as *maichou*. Textbooks for the hills were printed in the Roman script.

It was during the 1920s and 1930s, in the immediate period before the Second World War, that Manipuri literature witnessed its renaissance through the works of pioneering writers like Hijam Ananghal (1892–1943), Sorokhaibam Lalit (1892–1955), Khwairakpam Chaoba (1893–1943),

Hawaibam Nabadwipchandra (1897–1946), Dr Lamabam Kamal (1900–1934), Ashangbam Minaketan (1906–1995), Arambam Dorendrajit (1907–1944), and Rajkumar Shitaljit (1913–2008) who used varied forms such as poetry, drama, the novel, the short story, the epic and literary criticism. This literary development was in part aided by the birth of many journals in this period like *Meitei Leima* (1914), *Meitei Chanu* (1922), *Jagaran* (1924), *Yakairol* (1930), *Lalit Manjari Patrika* (1933), and so on.

Works of local writers such as Khwairakpam Chaoba's *Chhatra Macha*, Ashangbam Minaketan Singh's *Basanta Seireng* and Arambam Dorendrajit's *Kangsa Bodh*, as well as translations like Ph. Vasudev Sharma's *Sakuntala* and M. Koireng Singh's *Kapal Kundala* came to be prescribed as textbooks for high school and college students. Other notable works of this period include Dr Lamabam Kamal's *Madhabi* (1930), the first Manipuri novel, Chaoba's *Labanga Lata* (1934), Anganghal's *Khamba Thoibi Seireng* and *Jahera* (published posthumously in 1964) and Rajkumar Shitaljit's *Thadokpa* (1942).

The 1930s also saw the establishment of many theatre houses such as Manipur Dramatic Union, Aryan Theatre and Society Theatre which staged plays in the vernacular, forsaking the earlier enactments in Bengali. Many writers like Sorokhaibam Lalit, Arambam Dorendrajit, Ashangbam Minaketan and Hijam Anganghal started exploring historical and mythological themes and wrote popular plays like *Sati Khongnang* (1930), *Moirang Thoibi* (1935), *Poktabi* (1935), *Sita Banabas* (1936). Playwrights like Haobam Tomba (1908–1976), M. Biramangol (1909–1979), L. Netrajit (1914–1992), Meitram Bira (1916–1978), Sarangthem Boramani (1928–2013) explored themes related to Manipuri folk culture, legends and patriotism in plays like *Haorang Leisang Saphabi*, *Yaithing Konu*, *Puya Meithaba* and *Bir Tikendrajit*.

At this juncture, Janneta Hijam Irabot (1896–1951) emerges as a revolutionary figure in the socio-political and literary scene of Manipur. A firm believer in the upliftment of women, the eruption of the Second Nupi Lan in 1939 led him to form a new political party – Manipur Praja Sammelini – to support the women's movement. Irabot, who was soon after arrested for organizing public meetings wherein he spoke out against the government, was also a poet, actor and journalist. He published a number of journals including *Meitei Chanu* and *Anouba Yug*. Among his notable works are the anthology of poems, *Sheidam Sheireng* (prescribed as a school textbook) and travelogue essay, *Mandalay Khongchat*. However, it was his poems, 'Shillong' and 'December Taranithoi' in his book *Imagi Puja* (published posthumously in 1987) written during his imprisonment in Sylhet Jail that stand out for their honest depiction of Manipuri women's status and condition. In these poems, he deviates from the hitherto existing stereotypical representation of women as patient, enduring, forbearing and sacrificing people. Instead, he portrays the condition of women as that of caged slaves trapped in an oppressive domesticity under a tyrannical husband, and asks when they will get their independence. This is Irabot's pioneering worldview that upholds the idea that women should have an equal footing and importance in society.

The period after the Second World War saw the emergence of a new elite group of traders and businessmen. The changing value system which laid more emphasis on materialistic achievements in lieu of traditional morality, further tightened the noose around the idea and concept of womanhood. Though many writers like Elangbam Nilakanta (1927–2000), Laishram Samarendra (1925–2016), Hijam Guno (1926–2010) emerged during this period, it was GC Tongbra (1913–1996) and Arambam Somorendro (1935–2000) who questioned the traditional value systems around womanhood in their plays.

Women Writers in Manipuri Literature

Even though male writers had laid a solid foundation for New Manipuri Literature by this time, women were still unable to make a foray into the world of literature.

The delay was mainly due to the late introduction of schools for girls and the obstacles placed by society, tradition and belief systems on girls' education. The first LP school for girls set up at Moirangkhom (now in Imphal West District) in December 1899 had to close down within a year due to widespread rumours that the girls would be shipped off to England as soon as they were able to read and write. Though a few elite women could get a partial education through home tutors, it was only in 1935 with the establishment of the Tamphasana Girls High School that more girls started coming to school. However, they had to endure widespread scorn, bullying and harassment to do so. By this time the male writers had grouped together to form the Manipuri Sahitya Parishad.

The Pioneers: Thoibi, Binodini and Pramodini

Among the first few women who were fortunate to receive an education, three prominent figures, Takhellambam Thoibi (1920-1996), Maharajkumari Binodini (1922–2011) and

Khaidem Pramodini (1924–2006) emerged as pioneering women writers.

During their early years and throughout their lives, the vision and outlook of these three writers was shaped by firsthand experiences of the various transitions and historical events Manipur went through. They encountered the subjugation of a free people under British rule, saw the bravery of the women in the Second Nupi Lan and imbibed the communist ideals of Hijam Irabot. They experienced the death and horrors of the Second World War, the euphoria of independence from British rule in 1947, and the brief self-rule in Manipur as an elected democracy. Yet again, they went through the angst-filled times of the controversial 'merger' of Manipur into the new Indian nation-state in 1949, and saw the birth of various nationalistic insurgent movements in Manipur which led to widespread armed violence, the declaration of the state as a 'Disturbed Area' and the imposition of the Armed Forces Special Powers Act (1958). They also heard the many stories of army torture, massacres, rape and molestations and burning down of villages during counter-insurgency operations by government security forces.

By this time, the influence of Bengali literature was gradually fading. It was replaced by attempts to develop forms that were more representative of the local context and taste, and the changing environment in post-independent Manipur. Writers now began to move from the romantic and idealistic mode of writing to a kind of realism that focused on the dashed hopes of the people recently unyoked from colonial rule only to have a new nationhood imposed on them, the deteriorating social and financial conditions, the breakdown of traditional morality, the shift to materialistic values, the apprehension of changing times, and the pitiable conditions of the poor and downtrodden.

It was at this stage that Thoibi, Binodini and Pramodini – who came from different social and familial backgrounds – made their mark on the literary scene and explored different forms such as the short story, poems, novels and travelogues. Thoibi grew up unable to publicly acknowledge her Bengali father for fear of societal criticism. Binodini, as the daughter of Churachand Maharaj (1891–1941) and Maharani Dhanamanjuri also known as Ngangbi Maharani (1886–1975) grew up in the lap of luxury at the royal palace. As one among many daughters of a widowed mother, Pramodini grew up in an all-female family within the boundaries of a highly patriarchal society. A chord that bound them together was their familiarity and closeness to communism. Thoibi and Pramodini were compatriots and followers of Hijam Irabot. Binodini was introduced to communist thought through her friends during her early education in Shillong, and was later associated with the translation of Nihar Kumar Sarkar's book *Chotoder Rajniti* from Bengali into Manipuri as *Anganggi Rajniti* (Politics for Children).

Though these women were able to publish their writings, their journey was not without obstacles. Binodini had started writing early when she was in high school. But when she showed her first story 'Imaton', which explores the relationship between a young stepmother and her much older stepson, to her home tutor, he scolded her for writing a story (and at such a young age) on a theme that bordered on incest.

After this incident, Pramodini, whose education was sponsored by Queen Ngangbi, published three of Binodini's stories under her own name in the anthology

Punshi Meira (1958). By then, Pramodini had already established herself by editing *Kabi Tarpan,* an anthology of poems by male writers in 1950. She had also published *Nuja Phidam* (1951), which contained biographical sketches on the lives of extraordinary women, besides compiling and editing *Leimarol* (1957), another collection of stories on 'ideal women' drawn from the epics *Mahabharata* and *Ramayana*, as well as legendary women of Manipur.

Though from 1931, some women like Randhoni Devi, MK Binodini, Ramani Devi, Indu Devi and S Sarju contributed a few essays, poems or short stories to journals like *Yakairol, Lalit Manjari Patrika* and *Naharol*, the year 1965 is popularly regarded as the emerging point for women writers. It was in this year that Thoibi Devi's novel, *Radha* and MK Binodini's short story anthology, *Nunggairakta Chandramukhi* were published, making it the first instance of women writers showcasing their original and creative writings. Thus Thoibi is regarded as the first woman novelist of Manipur, while MK Binodini is renowned as the first woman short story writer in Manipur.

In their writings, all three delved deep into their experiences and socio-cultural milieu to portray the conditions of downtrodden men and women, while searching for an image that could define the ideal woman. Thoibi attempts to blend the ideals of the socially accepted image of woman with the mind of the new woman who had received a western education in her novels *Radha* (1965), *Nungshi Ichel* (1967), *Chingda Shatpi Ingellei* (1971) and *Lamja* (1973). Her vision progresses from the character of the traditionally approved, soft and gentle titular character in the novel *Radha* to that of an educated woman conscious of her likes and dislikes in her portrayal of the characters of Reena and Chitralekha in

Nungshi Eechel. Stopping short of defining the new woman, Thoibi's depiction of Dr Pratibha, who leaves behind the comfort of her town for the service of underdeveloped villages in *Chingda Shatpi Ingellei*, seems to denote the writer's holistic view of the socially-accepted ideal woman who also possesses the light of education and a modern outlook.

Despite being a princess who grew up in the royal palace, MK Binodini did not write about the privileges and luxuries of kings and queens. Instead, she sketches the lives of the common people, the downtrodden and the ill-fated in her stories. It was not only her understanding of people's hearts, but also the beauty of her literary language that made Binodini's fiction poignant and powerful, putting her at par with the new group of emerging male writers of the time.

Binodini portrays women as she sees them – the maidservant serving in the palace, the divorced woman trying to recover from a bad marriage, or the woman given the worse cards of fate. She does not comment or try to build up an ideal, but carefully builds up a scene or character and leaves it wide open for the reader's interpretation. As an artist and sculptor, Binodini's forte is in building up the character's heart and life, and touching the heart of the reader in doing so.

With the historical novel, *Bor Saheb Ongbi Sanatombi* (1976), based on the life of Surchandra Maharaj's daughter Princess Sanatombi, Binodini became the first woman writer of the state to receive the coveted Sahitya Akademi award in 1979. Through the character of Sanatombi, she depicts not only the highest strength of love which can cross boundaries of society, class and caste, but also beautifully illustrates the pangs and sufferings of the women kept unequal by societal and traditional norms.

Pramodini's writings were closely related to her upbringing in an all-women family at a time when women were very much looked down upon, and her own work as Director of the Women and Children Programme in the Manipur Government's Development Department. Collecting the biographies of renowned and exemplary women, she published *Nuja Phidam* (1951) and *Leimarol* (1957) trying to instil strength and wisdom in women. In her plays and novels, too, her aim is to empower and make the suppressed women think.

All three women were also very multifaceted writers foraying into translations, travelogues, drama, prose, poetry, short stories, novels, radio plays, screenplays, lyrics and memoirs. Pramodini even put out comic books – *Tok-nga Makhum Hangba* (1994) and *Tok-nga Charong* (1996). Notable among her writings are the travelogues *Echrishatki Collie Nupi* (1991), *Torbunggi Tera Pambida Shatpa Meibul* (1993), *Iben Mayo gi Lei Pareng* (1996) and *Huntre Hunpham Manipur* (2001), which narrates the lives of the people in the remote corners and hills of Manipur. Some of her other works are the poetry collections *Khorjeigi Manglan* (1983), *Loijing Loiya Seirenglei* (1984) and *Thingel Laija Iraokhol* (1984); short story collections *Palem Leipak Leima* (1984) and *Mukta Pareng* (1996); and novel *Kanglaba Sanarei Mayom* (1996). She also wrote a number of dramas and film scripts besides essays on culture and the arts.

Well versed in Bengali, Thoibi was the first woman in Manipur to receive the Sahitya Akademi Translation Award for her translation of Jajabor's (Binoy Mukhopadhay) novel *Dristipat* (1969) from Bengali into Manipuri. She also became the first woman writer to pen an autobiography with the publication of *Ningshinglakli Ngasida* in 1997. Predominently a novelist, she tried her hand at short stories and prose too, coming up with the collections *Post Mortem* (1980) and *Mityeng Ama* (1983).

Among Binodini's notable works are the radio play *Ashangba Nongjabi* (1967), which explores the limitless mind of an artist, her translation of Badal Sircar's *Evam Indrajit* from Bengali into Manipuri, a travelogue *Ho Mexico* (2004) and her memoir *Churachand Maharajgi Imung* (2008), which is notable for its depiction of the royal household. She also wrote a number of lyrics, besides scripts for award-winning feature films, ballets and documentary films. Both the films *Imagi Ningthem* and *Ishanou*, which she scripted (directed by Aribam Shyam Sharma), became internationally renowned. *Imagi Ningthem* won the prestigious *Montgolfiere d' Or* (Grand Prix), the top award at the 'Festival des 3 Continents, Nantes' in 1982, becoming the first Indian film to bag the award. The film *Ishanou* was the Official Selection (Un Certain Regard) for the Cannes Film Festival, 1991.

THE SECOND GENERATION

The work done by these three pioneering women writers was carried forward by a new generation of writers like Dr Chongtham Jamini (1936-), Sanjembam Bhanumati (1948-2001), Binapani Thokchom (1949-), Khummanlambam Sorojini (1951-), H Benubala (1951-), Khwairakpam Anandini (1952-), Longjam Ongbi Ibempishak (1953-), Haobam Satyabati (1953-), Chongtham Ongbi Subadani (1955-), Arambam ongbi Memchoubi (1955-), Haobam Nalini (1956-), Moirangthem Borkanya (1958-), Lairenlakpam Ibemhal (1958-), Chandrakala Tongbram (1959-) and Kshetrimayum Subadani (1959-), among many others.

Although they came from diverse backgrounds, many among the new wave of women writers belonged to the early batches of educated women. Some among them, like Sanjembam Bhanumati came from an artistic background (her father was a poet, singer and theatre artist), while others like Dr Chongtham Jamini and Binapani Thokchom grew up in a family which encouraged education and progressive thought. Binapani's father was the first doctor of Manipur while Jamini's father (and brothers) held high positions in the government. Many among them were highly educated (Jamini, Memchoubi and L. Ibemhal hold PhD degrees), and were employed in government departments and other organised sectors. At the same time, there were also others like Moirangthem Borkanya who grew up amidst hardships in an impoverished and broken family.

They not only represented the new middle class of the society which had risen after the Second World War, but also represented the new women – educated women negotiating with the boundaries of traditional patriarchal society and forging a new path. Growing up during the tumultuous transitional period in the history of Manipur between its status as a union territory in 1956 and statehood in 1972, they witnessed the intensification of insurgency in the state and the emergence of women as important socio-political actors – either as prohibitionists like the Nishabandh movement or as protectors of their community like the Meira Paibi and Tangkhul Shanao Long (TSL) collectives. They also experienced firsthand how the existing notions of women's honor and morality became tied up with national or social identity due to patriarchal society's sense of the loss of nationhood and identity.

Through their works, they examined their own conditions and status within the prevailing socio-political and traditional framework of their lived experiences. Some among them like Khwairakpam Anandini who published the first poetry collection among the women writers (*Sajibu Leirang*, 1967) and Sanjembam Bhanumati continued to adhere to socially accepted ideals of womanhood and tried to closely nurture notions of traditional morality – complying with the model of Sita as the enduring female spirit in the face of utmost suppression and oppression. This model of the ever-suffering and patient woman who suffers many times at the hands of society, family and husband but remains determined in her conviction to follow a righteous, traditionally-approved and sacrificing path is a recurring leitmotif in the works of many writers – male or female.

Yet at times there are sparks of rebellion. Even the romantic traditionalist Bhanumati pondered over women's predicament and was compelled to ask,

> Where is a daughter's home?
> Where is my true homestead?
> Will I leave without knowing it?
> Depart thus, baffled and lost?
> ('Kadaidano Ningol Iyumbo': *Aroiba Wahang*, 2001)

Dr Chongtham Jamini, who had already started writing school textbooks on physical education as early as 1961, serves as a bridge of sorts between the first three pioneers – Thoibi, Pramodini and Binodini – and the second generation of women writers. She was instrumental in shaping the minds of many from the new generation of women through her classroom where she frequently talked about the prevalent gender stereotypes and prejudices within the tradition, customs and religion. Further, she has also continued to question these through the literary work undertaken by her later in her life. For instance, in her short story, 'Chakkhum Palli' she questions the concept of purity and impurity in connection to menstruation, whereas the protagonist Maipakpi in the story, 'Changyeng' challenges the patriarchal notion of child-rearing and home-making as the sole responsibility of women.

At the same time, Jamini's longing to preserve certain beautiful aspects of tradition and culture is seen in her critical works on cultural history like *Khuroi Haoba Lamlangtong* (2004), *Shijalaioibi Amasung Maha Raas* (2005) and *Rasheshori Palagi Parampara* (2009), as well as in her stories like 'Taningdraba Sur', which depicts the aged protagonist, Thambalmarik's desire for her daughter-in-law to observe the Sajibu Cheiraoba (Meitei New Year) in accordance with the traditional customs.

Jamini, who was also the first Chairperson of the Manipur State Women's Commission (2006-2009), is a prolific travelogue writer producing works like *Swargagi Leibaktuda* (1994), *Korouhanbana Ironnungdagi Khongdoirakpa Lamduda* (1998), *Kohinoorgi Masaigonda* (2001), *Americagi Khongchat* (2001), *Akashi Gangagi Torbanda* (2009) and *Surdhuni Gangagi Mapanda* (2013). Her other works include the short story collections *Combing Operation* (1996), *Loinaidraba Wari* (1990), *Nungshi Khudol* (2006) and *Chekladugi Aroiba Bidai* (2010), and poetry collections *Leinam Chendrabasu Leirang Satli* (2008) and *Taro Warise Shinaigang* (2013).

Other women writers of this period also started voicing their angst at being bound by the traditions, customs and religion.

Ksh. Subadani tries to break down the ideals of womanhood in her books *Nahakpu Eigi Kanano* (1982), *Nunggi Chinbal* (1987) and *Pi Gi Wari* (1995). She starts critically exploring stronger women characters like Sanaibemma in 'Nunggi Chinbal' and Ibemnungshi in 'Yenningthana Lakpada'; the latter does not hesitate to break the bonds of marriage or deviate from societal norms in order to stand up for what she believes is right. Sanaibemma, who led an oppressed life because she could not bear a son, leaves her house when she is not given a say in the decision-making regarding her daughter's marriage. Ibemnungshi, ill-treated and neglected by her husband, is branded an 'immoral' woman for accepting the help of her husband's friend. Owing to certain events she briefly becomes a prostitute, but later establishes a business and starts living her life fully, as an independent woman.

Keenly aware of the pain-filled life that women led in the shadow of the idea of 'The Enduring Woman', the search for women's place between tradition and modernity spearheaded a gradual gendered consciousness of patriarchal morality. A new voice of women started building up through Arambam Ongbi Memchoubi's poems in her collections *Nonggoubi* (1984), *Androgi Mei* (1990), *Sandrembi Cheishra* (1993), *Eigi Palem Nungshibi* (1998), *Idu Ningthou* (2005), *Leisang* (2008) and *Tuphai O! Ningthibi* (2012). Memchoubi, who won the Sahitya Akademi Award in 2008, resists the image of the woman seated mutely on the pedestal of stereotypic ideals in her search for the concept of the new woman. She reviews the myth of the Nonggoubi bird who was denied drinking water as she did not join the communal work of dredging the river and canals because she was busy looking after her children. Opining that women's inability to enter decision-making bodies is due to their lack of political consciousness, she calls out to the Nonggoubi bird to join the creation of the new world.

> Come, come, O, Nonggoubi
> Today, the world will be created anew
> This journey is towards the light,
> Come, come, let's create together!
>
> ('Nonggoubi': *Nonggoubi*, 1984)

The new brand of women that Memchoubi envisages is, interestingly, not one based on a Euro-centric model. Rather, it is one drawn and sculpted from the roots of this land; it is the image of the Ultimate Mother. This is a decision she comes to after her decisive soul-searching journey. The image is not one of a dependent creeper, or a suppressed soul; it is the image of one doing her duty and claiming it as her responsibility.

> Inside the basket, in Mother's basket, I saw
> Her old husband,
> Her youthful son.
> Bewildered, I asked,
> 'Why Mother, what is this?'
> Mother looked at me once,
> And said slowly –
> 'If I don't carry them, how will they survive?'
> Without any further words,
> She walked away, as before,
> Calmly, solemnly,
> My beloved Mother.
>
> ('Eigi Palem Nungshibi': *Eigi Palem Nungshibi*, 1998)

A prolific writer, Memchoubi's other works include the short story collection *Leiteng* (1992), biography *Phou Charong* (1995), travelogue *Europagi Mapao* (2001), and critical essays *Wakma Maibi Amasung Atei Warising* (1999), *Haoreima Sambubi* (2000), *Amaibi: Manipurda Shamanism* (2006) and *Taungbo: Irawatki Aroiba Yahippham* (2015). She has also edited the anthologies *Manipuri Sahityada Nupigi Khonjen* (2003) published by Sahitya Akademi, New Delhi, and *Loilam Matunggi Manipuri Seireng* (2017) published by Aseilup, Manipur.

Lairenmayum Ibemhal (1958-) too urged for women's distinctive individuality, asserting that women are not mere shadows of men in her two poetry collections – *Leirol Chankhraba Thajaba* (1993) and *Nongthanggi Innaphi* (2002). In them, she deconstructs the image of the ever-suffering, enduring, traditional woman and calls for a reversal of roles.

> Like we slept together
> Every night
> Your liquor stench
> With
> My chinghi fragrance
> Let them roll together today
> My liquor stench
> With your body odour.
> Don't look at me thus
> This is no transformation to me
> Just that I have become you.
>
> ('Mami': *Nongthanggi Innaphi*, 2002)

The women writers felt strongly that it is women's own complicity that has given power to the customs and beliefs of patriarchal society and has made them unable to believe in themselves, and centuries of conditioning have allowed such ideas to take root in their very souls. Rejecting this tradition passed down from generation to generation by women themselves, L. Ibemhal calls it an oppressive dog-leash, and rejects this tyrannical practice.

> Therefore
> I've cut off thus today
> That which you all have forcibly
> Made into a murderous rope
> This noose around my neck.
>
> ('Konggoi': *Nongthanggi Innaphi*, 2002)

Strongly influenced by the wave of modernism in the Manipuri literary arena during the late nineteen sixties and seventies, Moirangthem Borkanya (1958-) started out as a novelist and was awarded the Sahitya Akademi Award for her novel *Leikangla* in 2010. But it is her powerful poetry in her collections *Loinaidraba Thawaigi Eshei* (1988), *Utol Amadi Ucheksing* (1991), *Shangbannaba Atiyagi Epaktei* (1995), *Yenningtha Nangna Khongdoi Hullakpasida* (2008) and *Henjunaha* (2018) that stands out for its stark portrayal of the struggles of women in a heartless society. Lamenting the distortion of women's selfhood, individuality and identity by patriarchy, she predicts that this oppression will not last forever, as from these oppressed hearts a revolution against the system will burst forth.

> Though for generations
> remained covered with a black veil,
> barred by mountains,

an unstoppable storm churns today
from thousands and thousands of hearts
of the images reflected in the shards of the broken mirror.
This rising storm is not in vain
it does not blow any other way, except yours
This tempest is aimed towards you
only towards you.

('Nongleise': *Yenningtha Nangna Khongdoi*
Hullakpasida, 2008)

THE THIRD GENERATION

This new awareness of women's condition in Manipuri society and the attempt to delineate a new place for women outside the subjugation of patriarchal, traditional and religious moulds was carried forward by the third generation of women writers who were mostly born between 1960 and 1980. Some among them are Ningombam Satyabati (1960-), Tonjam Sarojini (1960-), Maya Nepram (1960-), Bimabati Thiyam Ongbi (1960-), Koijam Santibala (1960-), RK Sanahanbi (Likhombi) Chanu (1962-), Mufidun Nesha (1963-), Ningombam Sanatombi (1964-), Ningombam Sunita (1965-), Guruaribam Ghanapriya (1965-), Nee Devi (1968-) and Ningombam Surma (1973-).

Growing up within an atmosphere of modernism, nationalism and violent conflict, they witnessed the further deterioration of the social fabric, the sharpening divide among communities, widespread violence, lack of accountability, ethnic clashes, and extra-judicial killings by both the underground and state armed forces.

By the mid-1990s the culture of silence on rape and sexual assault was beginning to lift, especially in cases where personnel from the army were the perpetrators, as many women became more outspoken and demanded justice. At the same time, many insurgent groups started addressing the issue of women's status, traditional morality and gendered violence – some by punishing those accused of rape and other forms of sexual violence, others by issuing dress codes for women, and yet others by banning the screening of Bollywood Hindi films on the grounds that the native values, morals and culture, especially for women, were being eroded by its influence. Simultaneously, a strong wave of women's activism prevailed with women's organizations such as the Naga Women's Union, Manipur (NWUM), Tangkhul Shanao Long (TSL) and Meira Paibi taking on the role of peacemakers and guardians of the land.

It was during this period of transition and contradictions that the literary wave of women writers which had surged in and around the urban areas of Imphal surfaced in other parts of the state. From Thoubal emerged four powerful writers who made their mark with their distinctive styles – Sunita Ningombam, Surma Ningombam, Sanatombi Ningombam and Satyabati Ningombam. Among them, Sunita Ningombam won the Sahitya Akademi Award with her debut collection of short stories *Khongji Makhol* in 2001. Writers like Naorem Romina and N. Pramodini came up in Kakching, while Kh Ibeton (1947-) emerged in Bishnupur. In the northern side, from the Awang Potshangbam circle emerged writers like RK Sanahanbi and Tonjam Sorojini.

At the same time, writers from other ethnic communities of Manipur emerged in the literary scene which had been mainly dominated by writers from the Meitei community. Leimiwon made her mark by becoming the first Tangkhul woman writer with her novels *Khipawui Khayon, Part-1* (1995), *Khipawui Khayon, Part-2* (1998), *Tangkhul Avaram* (2005), *Maranao Mirin* (2006) and *Iram Wonra* (2007) written in the Tangkhul language. *Siroy Chingjao*, published in 2008, is her first collection of short stories written in the Manipuri language and script. Mufidun Nesha (1963-) and N. Nesha came up as writers from the Manipuri Muslim community.

Together these women writers – both old and new – started searching for a place to let their individuality bloom freely. Raising their voices against restrictive and gender-biased customs, they began to explore new ideas such as women's rights, equality between genders, and so on. They also started approaching many hitherto unaddressed themes and aspects of the relationship between men and women, along with related social norms – such as the loss of women's individuality within a marital bond, the sexuality of women, and the relationships of transgender/non-binary individuals.

Thus, Bimabati Thiyam Ongbi, who began her literary foray with the short story collections *Khongchat* (1992) and *Etheikhraba Eechel* (2013), started reappraising relationships between men and women, the dynamics between husband and wife in a marriage, and the personal feelings of a woman. She beautifully delineates the fear of the loss of a woman's individuality within the quicksand of domesticity and the bonds of marriage in 'Wakat', the determined stand of a young widow to struggle on her own without seeking help in 'Eetheikhraba Eechel', and a mother's budding maternal love for her child in 'Khongthang' and 'Seihou'.

In Ningombam Satyabati's short story 'Amangba Nonglakki Nongthang', a peon's wife, Sanahanbi, angered by the frequent partying of the officers at their house during holidays, demands that Sunday be her holiday too. Sanatombi Ningombam explores the struggles of a woman trying to rise above the sundry and never-ending household chores and domestic responsibilities in order to express her creativity in her short story, 'Nupigi Sahitya'.

Maya Nepram's stories, in her collections *Wakat* (2004) and *Ngangleinaba Ithak Ipom* (2010), also reflect the consciousness of the new generation of women who are not afraid to make a conscious decision through characters like Thambal in 'Yanthatpikhraba Upal' – who sells liquor even though she knows she can be shot and punished by underground insurgents – just so she can meet her insurgent son in the process; or the character of the young widow Thourani in 'Churungngo Nangsu', who refuses to cry at the death ceremony of her alcoholic and womanising husband.

The women writers of this generation also start addressing issues related to the sexuality of women and gender identity. Even if they are unable to go beyond socially-accepted boundaries, their stories are first instances when women writers start to look beyond the existing tropes of the suffering mother, the enduring wife of an oppressive husband, the righteous widow and the fickle, unruly, wanton woman. This is evident in Sunita Ningombam's portrayal of the young widow Lalita in her short story 'Sendol Shingba', who finds herself physically attracted to the sensuality of a man, and yet chooses to forsake her new sensual realisation for the memory of her dead husband's love.

Nee Devi, who starts out as a novelist and poet with her two novels *Kadaidano* (1987) and *Cheithengpham* (1988), and the poetry collection *Chakngai Warisida* (1995), starts questioning the issue of gender disparity and the importance of women taking a stand in life in her short story collections *Shollaba Mari* (2001), *Lei Mana Amatang* (2009). She also sensitively approaches the issue of transgender relationships and the social stigma and discrimination surrounding those who identify themselves outside the socially accepted gender binary.

In her short story 'Manglaknaba', two biological women choose to live together but familial pressure and opposition force Leishna to buckle and start seeing a man instead, after which her partner Somorani commits suicide. In 'Leikangda Nanthuba', on realising that her husband identifies as a woman, Anjana rejects him/her and the marital bond just a few days after the wedding.

Among the many women writers coming from Manipuri settlements outside the state, Sorokhaibam Gambhini (1971-) from Tripura also notes the way women are kept trapped by the net of traditions within patriarchal society and poses many questions in her works, *Hanglakkanu Wahang Ado* (2001), *Bidai! Kangleipak Bidai* (2007) and *Yachangba Nang Hallo* (2018).

AFTER THE 80s

Haobijam Chanu Prema (1981-), Akhom Yandhibala (1981-), Angom Sarita (1982-), Konthoujam Ranjita, and so on belong to the newly emerging generation of women writers. Among them Konthoujam Ranjita, Akhom Yandibala and Angom Sarita are recipients of the Sahitya Akademi's Yuva Puruskar Award. Ranjita received the award for her short story collection, *Shingnabagi Ka Amasung Dairy Gimapu* in 2012, Yandibala received it in 2013 for her poetry collection, *Lai Matha Shaari,* while Sarita got it in 2015 for her poetry collection, *Mee Amashung Shaa.*

Among the younger poets, Haobijam Chanu Prema stands out with her unique style that blends wit, satire and dramatic narrative with a strong awareness of women's lives and sufferings in rural Manipur in her poetry collections, *Angangba Eeshing* (2007) and *Punshi Khongchatsida* (2011). Drawing deeply from her own childhood in a primarily agrarian and fishing community, she explores issues such as the social conditioning of a young girl's mind as per patriarchal norms, domestic violence, the socio-economic and political roles of a woman, menstruation and the social taboos surrounding it, and so on. Simultaneously, she starts questioning those social norms and responsibilities that treat women differently.

Another aspect of this period is the emergence of young women writers who write in English, such as Yuimi Vashum who talks about child sexual abuse and sexuality in her poetry collection, *Love.Lust. And Loyalty* (2018), and Linthoi Chanu who reappraises the Meitei myths in her collection of stories, *The Tale of Kanglei Throne* (2017).

The rich culture and diversity of Manipur has always provided fertile soil for the creative imagination of writers, both local and foreign. Even though it has been just a little over five decades since the emergence of women writers, their contribution to Manipuri literature has been immense in terms of the diversity of forms they have explored and the uniqueness of their approach. There hasn't been any aspect of life in Manipur that they haven't touched upon – whether it is romantic love, the beauty of nature found here, the tussle between modernity and tradition, the plight of the downtrodden, the impact of the ongoing armed conflict on the common people, migrants, gender issues, and so on. In fact, they go a length further and approach these topics with a uniqueness and sensitivity found only in women.

REFERENCES

Nahakpam Aruna. 2001. *Nongthangleima Amasung Taibang*. Imphal: Published by Chungkham Yashwanta Singh.

Ch. Manihar Singh. 1996. *A History of Manipuri Literature*. Delhi: Sahitya Akademi.

Girls' Hostel
Sri Bhavana

BINODINI

Translated from the Manipuri by
L. SOMI ROY

Celebrations for Rabindranath's 125th anniversary are going on this year. I, too, am thinking of Gurudev. His literature, his songs, and life in his ashram. What I remember constantly today is Sri Bhavana, the hostel that was the living quarters for all the girls. The building was not very large. It had two storeys. All the girls from every department lived in this hostel. In those days, there were not that many people. It was the first time in my life that I had lived in a hostel. Upon admission, I was put right away in a long room with six girls. I found it uncomfortable. But slowly I met some women I liked. And I made one or two very close friends.

I took part in the *beitalik*, the procession of singers, the first thing early every morning. Drums, gongs, and cymbals in hand, I was among the many who wandered around the ashram. I loved it. Whether one knew the words to the songs or not, we sang out loud:

> Joyo hok
> Nobo arundoi joyo joyo
> May the new rays of the sun prevail
> May they prevail

What a wonderful way to start a new day! We got to know ourselves through the songs of Gurudev, among the mango blossoms, among the autumn leaves. The message of his songs made us love, made us fall in love. And we heard someone sing:

> You will never know
> In what strange ways the bond of melody
> Has bound us together.
> You will never know
> What prayers have blessed me with you!

Some of us became close, then some of us drew apart. And I joined a group to my liking. There were four of us. We came from different lands, we spoke different tongues, we looked different. One was Malayali, one was from Orissa, another from Assam, and I, a Manipuri. But we were all students of Kala Bhavana. We had all come from distant lands to learn to paint and sculpt. And so, we were especially close. Satchels slung on our shoulders, we wandered all over the place to do our sketching. We moulded clay and made sculptures together. We learned to make garlands, needles in hand.

The one we loved the most in our group was the Malayali maiden. She was the seniormost among us. She had already been there before us. They also said she was sent by the Kasturba Gandhi Trust. And that she used to be a professor of Carnatic music. She was a person of great quality, not like us. She truly seemed to be a maiden of the ashram, and so we called her 'Shakuntala', though she never knew that we did.

Every morning she would have a bath, and then, with her loose hair falling freely below her waist, she would tidy up the studio of the Master, Nandalal Bose. She would put one or two blossoms of flowers in season – singgarei, bokul, champa – in the clay pot that he used to put water in for his painting, so that even the water he worked with was scented.

I am thinking of her today. How lovable was that comely, dusky maiden. But she was not like the rest of us. Sometimes she would draw away from us. She was beyond our reach. She never once joined us when we ate the *amla* fruit we had brought down from the trees, or the small green mangoes we gathered that we dipped in salt and ate. We gave her a share of our mangoes, *amla* and *ber*. She pickled them in jars and placed them in a row in the sun on the windowsill in her single room. We used to creep into her room at odd moments and pinch them. But she never found out, for she was oblivious to trivial matters such as this. We delighted in her never catching us at our thievery.

She wore many beautiful clothes from Kerala. She always wore them neatly and with discernment. Her adornment was not colours but purity. And she often let down her black tresses. There was one stole that she wore now and then. How I loved it, how I coveted it…. I borrowed it from her every now and then. At some point, when I had borrowed it so frequently from her, I began to think it belonged to me. I began to put it away carefully in my closet. I thought to myself that I looked very fetching when I wore it with my striped embroidered *phanek*. The stole was white with a broad border of gold.

Once Sarojini Naidu came to our convocation at Visva-Bharati. There was a huge reception. Word came to Sri Bhavana: send some girls to give flowers to Sarojini, and include that Manipuri girl too. She must wear her national dress, and so on. They must have liked our *phaneks* a great deal.

So, for this occasion, I put on my *phanek* of *chigonglei* blossom gold, wore that stole, and was among the girls who offered flowers to Sarojini Naidu. How pretty I looked that day, I thought to myself… But alas, it seems that once, on another occasion, my friend caught a girl we knew wearing that stole together with my *phanek* that she had taken behind my back.

Shakuntala left us, heartbroken, all of a sudden one day. It was a personal matter. We were saddened at our parting, but we felt deep inside that it would not do to be loud and create a scene. We seemed to say:

> You have left us
> Leaving behind
> This song of spring

Sundays were not a holiday at Santiniketan. Every Wednesday there was a meeting with songs and prayers by the people at the ashram. After the worship, everyone went their own way. The four of us used to go off together. Since Shakuntala knew how to sing, she often sang solos. But on many a Wednesday, she would not come with the rest of us. She took a different path and went off on her own. We never asked her about it; we never thought to ask. But I heard some say that she was deeply in love at that time with one of the professors, a great scholar.

An incident one day. A crowd of people huddled in her single room. There was a doctor; there were nurses and women teachers. We were not allowed in. But I heard her weeping inside. People began to talk quietly. My Shakuntala had been deserted by Dushyanta the scholar. He had deceived her.

Things quietened down. One day, not long after, I went to her in her room. I found her with her hair down, singing softly with her *veena* in her lap.

Listen to the song
Of Ram Nidhu

When she saw me, she laughed and said, 'I am fine, it is quite all right.' With the impetuousness of youth, I cried out, sobbing loudly, 'I will kill him.' But she had calmed down. She had gathered herself. With a little smile, she put her arms around me.

Shakuntala left us. The day she left was the last time we saw her. The letter she wrote to the three of us, we took turns to keep under our pillows. But her letter three months later carried a different tune. It took us by surprise. It said, '… I am terribly in love with someone. I am so happy.…' We laughed. What a love addict! Then the thought struck us, what if the man she says she is in love with was Dushyanta the scholar? Had they gotten back together? No, that did not seem likely. We still saw him now and then in the ashram. Whenever our paths crossed, he tried to reach out to us, to talk to us, but we used to turn our faces away and walk off. We never even looked back at him.

Not long after, we each got a wedding invitation card from our beloved friend. A few years later, after I was living in Manipur, she wrote to me, 'I have given birth to a son. Do you know the name I have given him? I have named him after you – Binod.' Binod, Binod! How thrilled I was. But she did not live long. Yes, it is true, she was made to live in the heavens. An officer who knew her came to Manipur one day and I learnt of her death from him, 'She died of cancer. Didn't you hear? It was in all the papers.' But she lives. And I wonder how big her son is now. Would he be dusky like his mother? Would he have his mother's gentle gaze?

But, Binod ... Binod, my child. You will not know that in a distant mountain land, lives a friend of your mother.

Binod, Binod.

This short narrative was published in the Manipuri daily *Poknapham* on 19 February 1987. Today, the hostel is called Sri Sadana. A working draft of the translation was published in *The Vishva-Bharati Quarterly* in 2016. Copyright L. Somi Roy, Imasi: The Maharaj Kumari Binodini Devi Foundation © 2018.

Kitchen Duty

CHONGTHAM JAMINI DEVI

Translated from the Manipuri by
THINGNAM ANJULIKA SAMOM

Ekashini has been complaining since early morning. She grumbles non-stop as she sweeps the room … as if she wants her sleeping husband to hear her.

'How lazy men can be! All these household chores – sweeping, mopping the floors, fetching water, washing clothes, cooking food – everything is supposed to be women's responsibility. But men don't even acknowledge all the work that women do, or even how hard it is', she mutters aloud.

Ekashini continues, 'Fine, leave all that aside! But there are so many rules society binds us with – women can and can't do this or that; this is impure, that is pure … every month there are other restrictions – she can't touch such and such clothes, cook or fetch water.'

Interrupting her tirade, little Bobo calls out, 'Ima, I'm late for tuitions. Give me my pants and shirts, and also my tiffin.'

'You're big enough now. Do some of your own work, Ibungo, my boy. Take your clothes from the cupboard and get dressed. As for tiffin, it's your father's turn to make it today. But he's not awake yet so go, wake him up and negotiate with him.'

Then she returns to her monologue. 'These laws and customs made by men continue to bind women. And also hand over so many duties to women! Rearing a child is also a woman's job, they say. Just tell me, nowadays, is it possible for a woman to bring up a child all alone? The things that these children see and hear around them these days! Surely, all that has an influence on them', she continues her harangue as she mops the floor.

Ibochouba is still in bed. But he overhears all that his wife has been spewing. He turns on his side and calls out, 'Pemma, my dear! Got some more corn to pop? Finish it and let me get up. And hand me a cup of tea, will you?' That only seems to infuriate Ekashini more. She raises her voice and replies with exaggerated politeness, 'Since I cannot enter the kitchen, I won't be able to make the tea today. Please do get up quickly, and be the cook today.'

Ibochouba exclaims, 'Ha! What did you say? Me? And cooking?'

'Yes, today it's Dear Father's turn in the kitchen. It's getting late for the children's school. Food has to be ready in time for them. Do get up', Ekashini says.

She continues, 'What's to be done? In our society, we women have to dance to the tune of men's drumbeats. When our monthly periods come, we are regarded as untouchables and barred from the kitchen. We are called impure and not allowed to even touch many things. Didn't you say that? Since this woman is an untouchable these days, Dear Father, you being the pure one, you'll have to cook today.'

Ibochouba retaliates, 'You women! Just for some insignificant work like cooking, how much you whine! The saying goes, when you have tongs, you don't use your hands to hold the fire – that's why, otherwise…! Just you wait now. I'll cook, and it'll be so tasty that you'll bite off your lips and tongue. You'll be left licking your fingers.'

Ibochouba bathes. Wrapping a freshly-washed *khudei* around his waist, he enters the kitchen. As soon as he goes in, the commands fly out one after another.

'Do you hear, Bobo's Mother?'

'Yes?' Ekashini enters.

'Come. Give me what needs to be cooked.'

'Please choose from the vegetable basket and do what you have to.'

'How cunning is this woman!'

'What can I do? Since I am impure and untouchable, I can't touch the vegetables', Ekashini replies sharply.

'If you can't, call the child.'

'He's studying.'

'Eka! Today you'll surely get a beating.'

Ekashini marches out without a word.

Ibochouba has no choice now. Upholding customs and traditions, he has to cook. Seating his plump body on a *mora*, he rummages in the vegetable basket and takes out some mustard leaves and hooker chives. Then he starts preparing them intending to make mustard stew. He scoops out rice from the *chengphu* pot and without considering whether the water measure in the cooking pot is adequate or not, he pours in a big amount of the rice into the water. Covering the pot, he lowers the heat, putting it to a simmer.

Heating up oil in another pot, he drops the hooker chives from almost a standing position onto the hot oil, making flames erupt. '*Jou, prok, prok*', the herbs sizzle. A piece of the hooker chives bursts up from the pan and lands on his cheek.

'This just isn't a doable task', he mumbles to himself, stroking his cheek.

Previously, whenever she had her monthly periods and couldn't enter the kitchen, Ekashini would engage Sumati, their niece living next door, to cook for them. Today Sumati had gone to help out with the wedding arrangements of a cousin. She was going to stay there till the big feast on the fifth day after the wedding. There's no one else who can be persuaded to cook for them, so Ibochouba has to take on kitchen duty today, even though he has no previous knowledge that can help him perform this new role.

Ekashini enters the kitchen again. She comments loudly, stretching her words a bit, 'The rice seems overcooked; it smells burnt. The food's going to be so tasty that I'll be biting off the tip of my tongue.'

Ekashini's observation comes at that precise moment when Ibochouba is desperately nursing his teary eyes. A few seconds earlier he had rubbed an itch around his eyes with the same fingers that had been mashing chillies alongwith fermented fish for the side-dish. But he doesn't want his wife to know. He feels quite helpless. But, he says, nonchalantly, 'What do you know? Don't start your tirade here. I don't want to hear it.'

A call comes from outside, 'Bondhu, my dear friend, are you home?'

Without waiting for an answer, Tomchou rushes straight into the house. The level of intimacy between the friends is such that he makes a beeline for the kitchen without even pausing.

'Eh! Bondhu, what's this? How come you're so dutiful today? You, with ladle and tongs! And in the kitchen!'

Ibochouba replies, 'Bondhu, it's my turn in the kitchen today. Customs and traditions are quite a complicated thing.'

'Sure thing, they are! Yesterday when my wife, your sister-in-law Landhoni, went out for some work, a few friends had come over. I had to make the tea. When she returned, how she nagged, saying that I had finished a week's ration of tea and sugar, and that it was hard to scrub clean the pot charred from the milk spilling over! She ranted about so many things!'

The two friends come out to the verandah to continue the discussion. They both arrive at the unanimous conclusion – that from time to time, a man taking over kitchen duty is a good way to understand the hardships women face in taking care of household chores.

This short story was first published in Manipuri as 'Chakkhum Pali' in the collection of short stories *Chekladugi Aroiba Bidai*, written by Dr Chongtham Jamini Devi and published in 2010 by the author for Writers Forum, Manipur.

Adornments

AYUNG TAMPAKLEIMA RAIKHAN

Translated from the Manipuri by
NATASHA ELANGBAM

Let me renounce today all my adornments,
These earrings in my ears, this necklace around my neck,
For whom to come and look longingly
Do I carry this heavy burden of adornments?

Let me not wear these clothes,
Let my blood flow free,
With a freedom never known
Beyond shame and fear let it be seen by any who want to see.

Why is my chest bound so tight?
Is it a punishment for the milk that flows from these breasts?
Who hasn't drunk this milk?
Let it remain free like old times.

Who has thrown me this rag to veil myself?
I will not veil myself, do not gaze upon my feminine form.
It's your gaze, your desire,
My veil has nothing to do with you.

I touched your feet one day, in front of all
Tonight at this silent hour you suck my toes
Say whose feet are pure? Whose impure?
And what is purity, do let us hear?

Is it to immerse oneself in the Ganga for one's sins?
Is it one sinner begging another for forgiveness?
Is it the ferocious chants of an unknown language?
Or the purity concocted by the impure lot?

This poem was first published in Manipuri as 'Leiteng' in the anthology *Samjirei*, published in 2010 by the Leimarol Khorjeikol (Leikol), Manipur.

Where Is A Daughter's Home?

SANJENBAM BHANUMATI

Translated from the Manipuri by
SHREEMA NINGOMBAM

When I was a little girl,
When I wore my *phanek* below my navel,
With the *kumlang* earrings strung through my ears lobes,
In my father's big house
I had spent, thinking it my home –
I had thought wrong.

Along the golden roads
For the sake of my dearest beloved
Went thus I on my bridal palanquin;
There I made my home and birthed
Believing it all my eternal treasure –

When the master of the house passed away
The grand house with its huge rooms
Now belonged to our children;

I owned nothing,
I had thought wrong.

In the dusk of life,
When all I had was taken back from me,
When *Khamnung Kikwai Lou-Onbi*, the Goddess of Afterlife,
Beckons me like a mother
This little hut, newly built
By my children, grandchildren and neighbours
Has it become my true home?

Where is a daughter's home?
Where is my true homestead?
Will I leave without knowing it?
Depart thus, baffled and lost?

Written in 1998, this poem was first published in Manipuri as 'Kadaidano Ningol Iyumbo' in the anthology *Aroiba Wahang* in 2001, published by Maibam ningol Pukhrambam ongbi Devala Devi on behalf of PS and Tamra Publications, Manipur.

My Husband's Child

HAOBAM SATYABATI

Translated from the Manipuri by
AKOIJAM SUNITA

Modhu has been sitting in the verandah since early morning. He seemed to be deep in thought but it was hard to tell what he was thinking about. It is not clear whether it is joy or sorrow that he holds in his head.

Ibemcha leaves her cooking and hurries out from the kitchen. Wordlessly, she looks at her husband, and then goes back in again. Her mind in a state of turmoil and her whole body tense with anxiety, she seems unable to concentrate on the work at hand. She mutters incoherently. An uneaten plate of food, apparently from last night's dinner, is kept neatly in a corner of the kitchen.

Ibemcha comes out again. She looks at her husband and says, 'Where could the child have gone to? Please go and look around for him.'

'Where should I go looking for him? He's no longer a small

child in need of baby-sitting. He must have thought that he's man enough now and can take care of himself. That's why he left on his own. He'll come back eventually.'

Ibemcha is not happy with this reply. 'What if something untoward happens to the child, how can you be so indifferent?'

Modhu raises his voice slightly, 'Who should I ask about him then? Should I post something in the newspapers or inform the police?'

Infuriated, Ibemcha shouts back, 'If you can't find him, post it in the newspapers or go to the police. Without even a search, how will you find him? At least make a start by looking around for him.'

She turns swiftly and goes in. After a while, she announces from inside the house, 'Fine. All of you stay silent and do nothing. I'll go look for him.' She marches off to her room to change.

At this turn of events, Modhu calls out to his eldest son, 'Ibohal, why don't you go to his friend's place and see if they know where he is?'

'Paji, I've got some work. I'm late as it is. Perhaps Ibosana can go.'

Ibosana, studying for his upcoming matriculation exam, hears the exchange. In a derisive tone, he responds from his study table, 'The other day, Saphaba, from the northern neighbourhood, said that *he* talked about going back to his father's house.'

The whole discussion is happening within Ibemcha's hearing. A member of this family has not returned since yesterday, but no one seems worried or concerned. This is the reason behind this exchange of verbal volleys in the family. For her eldest son, his work is more important. The

61

middle son too only shares gossip, as if mocking everyone; while the father seems unaffected and nonchalant. It looks like the only person who is sick with worry is herself, Ibemcha, the mother.

After some very hard times, this family has only just started seeing better days. When Modhu and Ibemcha married, all their three children were already born. Ibemcha came to this house when Modhu's eldest son was a young boy. When she came, her own son was still a baby, slung piggyback onto her back.

Both man and woman had tied the cords of their lives together, being in sincere agreement with each other at the time. Together, they had vowed that she would love and nurture the two children who were already there at the house as if they were her own, and he had similarly said that he would love and nurture the little infant she had brought along as a real father ought to. Together they had decided that his children and her child were equally their children. During the time they had brought up the children together, they had ceased to be the weepy widow and the crabby widower. They had lived together as a family happily; but the two children who were already present at the house knew one thing – their new mother was not their biological mother and their youngest sibling came from somewhere else.

Human beings live together and form a society. And again this very society breaks human relations. This is a trap created and set up by humans themselves. Their youngest son did not come back to the house or to the parents. The father frequently says that he is a disobedient child and has caused untold pain to his parents. But everyday Ibemcha chants, 'My disobedient child, I'm waiting for you.' This constant anxiety about her son makes her lose interest in everything, even food, and slowly her health deteriorates.

At his wife's condition, Modhu remarks, 'Do you love only your biological child? Look how much these two children adore you. You do not seem to appreciate how they are serving you.'

Ibemcha doesn't reply. The gradual weakness soon makes her bedridden. The two remaining sons say, 'Ima, please don't worry. Tell us what you want.' Ibemcha doesn't utter a word. She just remains silent. There is a grievance deep inside her. She knows that her disobedient son was never like that earlier. Nobody knows this except for the mother's tiny heart.

When their eldest son Ibohal applied for a government loan, he was required to show land deeds. And the land deeds had to be in his name. Efforts were made to divide up the ancestral land so that he could inherit some of it and register it in his name. It was during this division that the conflict arose. The two elder sons said their youngest sibling need not get a share of the property. Modhu also proceeded to put this into action. At this behaviour, her son, who had barely left his tender child-like voice to start speaking in a manly voice, was deeply embarrassed. Ibemcha too was helpless. This being the cause, the once happy family had fallen out like oil and water. Today the family stands divided. One of their children has left home without a trace. The two others remain at home.

At these changing circumstances, Ibemcha too nursed some resentment towards Modhu – he had not treated the three children equally. What could she herself do, having left one place to come to another? A woman can stay as long as she has good relations with her husband; otherwise she has no place to go. This turmoil made Ibemcha's health decline with each passing day. Now she has become ill in the real sense; she can no longer get up from her bed. Even all the household chores are managed by the two sons. Doctors are called; traditional healers and astrologers are consulted. They all run around, doing whatever they can for Ibemcha but her health does not improve.

One day the eldest son rushes back home from work and informs the mother, 'Ima, I know where Mocha is. He seems to have gone back to his father's home at Sanjenbam Khunou village.'

The father overhears this. He says calmly, 'Very well, it's good if he has returned to his own house. Did you meet him?'

'No, Paji. Earlier in the day I saw him in the Dharamshala area, disembarking from a passenger bus that goes to Assam. I called out but he didn't hear and walked away. I couldn't catch up with him in the market crowd. I asked the bus driver and he told me that Mocha helps him out as a handyman.'

That concludes the discussion; no one says anything further. Lying on the bed, Ibemcha listens and waits eagerly. She hears her husband's words supporting her youngest son. But she isn't satisfied. She finds peace in knowing about her son's choice, but she does not agree with the one supporting this 'right' decision. Should she seek legal redress against him for not honouring the promise they had once made as widow and widower? What is happening is nothing less than sprinkling salt on a fresh wound. Ibemcha calls out from her bed, asking for someone to go and bring back her youngest son. He must have felt very hurt, she says. But who will go and bring him back– that is the problem.

For a long time now, Ibemcha has been restless, lost in a maze of thoughts. But today the turmoil seems to have ebbed, and she feels a calmness settling. She has arrived at a decision, even though the choice does not bring her any peace of mind. All the buried resentment, all the words that remained unspoken, and all acts of opportunism, she is familiar with all of these and has kept this knowledge hidden in a corner of her heart. Her health has improved a bit; she gets up and tightens her *khwangchet*, the strip of cloth tied around her waist which apparently gives her strength. She has been indoors for many days and looks pale, almost bloodless. She starts attending to a few household chores. Her husband says, 'Leave them. Don't do them if you're not feeling well.'

The words are said lovingly. Ibemcha shows no sign that she's heard and continues with what she is doing. A little later, her eldest son tells her, 'Ima, I'm going to the market. I'll look for some fish for you.' She doesn't respond.

It is late evening, just before dusk. The oppressive heat of the day has subsided, the cool breeze starts to wake up. In a while the sun will also go down behind the western hill range. Ibemcha changes her clothes and, coming up to Modhu, declares, 'I'm leaving.'

Modhu is astounded. The words hit him like an earthquake which leaves behind a trail of destruction and devastation within moments, turning a beautiful city into piles of debris. He cannot gather his thoughts. He looks on, bewildered by the sudden and unexpected change of events. Ibemcha does not wait for a response. She walks out slowly.

Ibemcha heads towards Top Yaral Konjil to reach Sanjenbam Khunou. The night calm has descended. Not even insects populate the roads and lanes; everything is silent. Ibemcha walks on all alone. Everything was shrouded in darkness – the tree tops and bamboo tops, even the Nongmaijing hill range was enveloped by the shadows. Ibemcha too has merged into the dark. The two ends of her *khwangchet* swaying rhythmically in the darkness, she crosses the Khewa Bridge. Though the dying light of the waning moon cannot create ripples in the lean Iril river, the water flows like melted silver. Using all the strength and resolve she has kept stored so far in this lifetime, she crosses Tinseed Road with weak steps. Yaral Pat too is left behind.

After several years Ibemcha finally reaches the homestead at Sanjenbam. Only the bare skeleton of the house remains, showing clearly that it is ownerless. There is no wall left standing, except in the upper part of the house where some remnants of a few walls stand precariously. There's not a door or window to be seen. The beams placed during the early construction of the house to hold up the roof are, however, intact. It looks like a place where children come to play during the day. The central portion of the house is almost washed white in the moonlight. Ibemcha walks in, exhausted, taking anxious steps. She climbs up to the porch and enters the house. In the dim moonlight she sees her son sleeping on an uneven bed, using his hand as pillow, his body curled up. She hears herself say, 'My dear son!'

Mocha opens his eyes wide. Surprised at seeing his mother standing there, he exclaims, 'Ima!'

Ibemcha steps closer and sits down besides her son. Mocha calls out again, softly this time, 'Ima!'

Ibemcha reaches out and touches her son, caressing him gently. Mocha also sits up. In the dying moonlight both mother and son gaze lovingly at each other. Then the son lies down slowly, placing his head on his mother's lap, snuggling up. Ibemcha holds him with both her hands. Far away, in the northwestern sky, the incomplete crescent moon shines crookedly, as if secretly watching the celebration of the mother-son reunion.

This short story was first published in Manipuri as 'Eigi Nupagi Macha' in the collection of short stories *Eigi Nupagi Macha*, written by Haobam Satyabati and published in 2005 by Khundrakpam Publications for Writers Forum, Imphal.

Nonggoubi[1]

ARAMBAM ONGBI MEMCHOUBI

Translated from the Manipuri by
THINGNAM ANJULIKA SAMOM

The rivers and lakes, and the ponds too
Its water rise full to the brim;
The dark rainclouds embrace the blue sky
Tightly into their bosom;
The green hilltops also
Hide behind the cloud-veils.
But, O, thirstful Nonggoubi
Why do you call again –
Ku   ku   ku!
The green paddy fields and meadows

---

[1] The greater coucal or crow pheasant (*Centropus sinensis*) bird, which in Manipuri creation myth, didn't take part in the dredging of the rivers as it was looking after its babies and household works. As punishment, it was not allowed to drink water from the rivers, lakes, and so on, and had to quench its thirst with only rain water.

The clear, vast sky too
All are in a frenzy, all swept away wildly
At your melodious, lovelorn call,
Ku   ku   ku!
Love is a never quenching thirst –
The more you drink, the more you long.
Come, come, O, Nonggoubi
Today, the world will be created anew
This journey is towards the light,
Come, come, let's create together!

This poem was first published in Manipuri as 'Nonggoubi' in the anthology *Nonggoubi*, in 1984 published by Arambam Samarendra on behalf of Meino and Khomdon Publications, Imphal.

My Beloved Mother

ARAMBAM ONGBI MEMCHOUBI

Translated from the Manipuri by
THINGNAM ANJULIKA SAMOM

Daughter of the Mountain Chief,
Quiet and peaceful as the deepest forests
Solemn as the sky-high mountains
Enduring as the Earth, my Mother of the Hills,
Palem Haobi, my Mother of the Hills.
A *kokshet* wrapped around her head,
A *khwangchet* tightened around her waist,
Her bare feet
Trod through the thorny grasses of the rocky hillside.
A heavy carrying basket slung onto her back,
Hills after hills,
Range after range,
On and on she climbed up,
On and on she crossed, and went on.

Fetching water from the deepest gorge, calm and fearless
She gathers leaves and roots for her meals,
At the remote, quiet, tiresome terraced field.
After digging up all four sides, heaving 'Hoi'
After shooing away the wild pigs and monkeys, shouting 'Hoi'
Crossing one steep hillside after another
She climbed up, and she climbed on.
Exhausted, she wiped her sweat away,
My Mother of the Hills.

One day I asked her –
'O, my beloved Mother of the Hills
Inside the basket on your back
What rests within?
Inside the load on your back
What have you put in?
Let me look just this once, Mother.'
She said, 'Here, take a look.'
And then bending over, she showed me the load on her back
Not for a moment did she, however, put it down.

I peeped in, curious to know what was inside,
Inside the basket, in Mother's basket, I saw
Her old husband,
Her youthful son.
Bewildered, I asked,
'Why Mother, what is this?'
Mother looked at me once,
And said slowly –
'If I don't carry them, how will they survive?'

Without any further words,
She walked away, as before,
Calmly, solemnly,
My beloved Mother.

This poem was first published in Manipuri as 'Eigi Palem Nungshibi' in the anthology *Eigi Palem Nungshibi*, in 1998 published by Arambam Samarendra on behalf of Meino and Khomdon Publications, Imphal.

The Salty Sea

ARAMBAM ONGBI MEMCHOUBI

Translated from the Manipuri by
THINGNAM ANJULIKA SAMOM

Have you ever seen the lotus blooming
In the salty sea, peacefully blossoming there?
Even if it is The Lord of the Waters
Its feet caressed by hundreds of rivers,
Even if gems and precious stones abound,
Have you ever seen the lotus blooming
In the salty sea, peacefully blossoming there?
At the foot of the gently sloping hills,
In the clear, sparkling spring waters of the hills
So shallow, so small,
In the little lakes by the hills and meadows
Let me bloom, peacefully, contented
To the rhythm of the fishing nets and music of fishing traps
Of some poor widow seeking to earn her livelihood,
When the season arrives

Amidst the innocent laughter of those young lovers
Coming to feast on lilies and lotuses
Let me bloom, peacefully.
When the season ends
Let me wither and fall to the vast waters, contented.
Have you ever seen the lotus blooming
In the salty sea, peacefully blossoming there?

This poem was first published in Manipuri as 'Thumhigi Samudra' in the anthology *Leishang* in 2008, published by Arambam Yoimayai, Imphal.

When the Apsaras Awakened

CHONGTHAM SUBADANI

Translated from the Manipuri by
SOIBAM HARIPRIYA

Today a clamour surrounds
Indra's Royal Court,
The sounds of yore
Aren't heard anymore:
The rhythm of the Apsaras' celestial dance
In tandem with it, the melody of their anklets.
Now they push open again and again
The vast and mighty gates of Indra;
It has been long that they've languished
Like prisoners in a dungeon,
Like the *singgarei* flowers that only bloom for a single night
Having lost the rights of motherhood.
When the Apsaras awakened
Today the clamour surrounds
Indra's Royal Court,

The sounds of yore
Aren't heard anymore:
The rhythm of the Apsaras' celestial dance
In tandem with it, the melody of their anklets.

This poem was first published in Manipuri as 'Meekap Thoklabada Apsara-sing' in the anthology *Diwaligi Meira Pareng* in 2009, published by Yendrembam Anganba, Imphal.

Shadow

LAIRENLAKPAM IBEMHAL

Translated from the Manipuri by
THINGNAM ANJULIKA SAMOM

No, don't be angry,
Don't be angry, beloved!
'Tis a little I drank
'Cos my friends coerced me.

Like we slept together
Every night
Your liquor stench
With
My *chinghi*
fragrance.

Let them roll together today
My liquor stench

With your body odour.
Don't look at me thus
This is no transformation in me
Just that I have become you.

This poem was first published in Manipuri as 'Mami' in the collection of poems *Nongthanggi Innaphi*, written by Lairenlakpam Ibemhal, published in 2002 by Lairenlakpam ongbi Gambhini Devi for the Writers Forum, Manipur.

The Noose

LAIRENLAKPAM IBEMHAL

Translated from the Manipuri by
THINGNAM ANJULIKA SAMOM

To my mother
By my grandmother
To my grandmother
By my great-grandmother
To my great-grandmother
By my great-great-grandmother
She too
By the one who birthed her
One after another
Through the buried
Many centuries
Entrusted
This *huigang*
This dog-leash
Like a newly-wed's necklace
On my neck

Calmly garlanding
My
Dear Mother
Said –
'This is your adornment!'
But
I disliked it
Could never agree to it
Because
I saw
Through the forcible misinterpretation
Of the significance of this ornament
How you all
To those many
Named them
As you wished, and
Dragged them
In whichever directions you choose
Like a loyal dog
Or
Like obedient bullocks yoked to a cart
Therefore
I've cut off thus today
That which you all have forcibly
Made into a murderous rope
This noose around my neck.

This poem was first published in Manipuri as 'Konggoi' in the collection of poems *Nongthanggi Innaphi*, written by Lairenlakpam Ibemhal, published in 2002 by Lairenlakpam Ongbi Gambhini Devi for the Writers Forum, Manipur.

Love

LAIRENLAKPAM IBEMHAL

Translated from the Manipuri by
THINGNAM ANJULIKA SAMOM

'Do you love me?'
'Yes, I do.'
'How much?'
'Does it have a limit?'
'It didn't,
But now it has a limit. Tell me,
From the house,
Is it to the quiet meadows?
From the meadows,
Is it to the restaurant cabins?
Or maybe,
From the cabin,
Is it to the secret bedroom?'

This poem was first published in Manipuri as 'Nungshiba' in the collection of poems *Nongthanggi Innaphi*, written by Lairenlakpam Ibemhal, published in 2002 by Lairenlakpam Ongbi Gambhini Devi for the Writers Forum, Manipur.

This Storm

MOIRANGTHEM BORKANYA

Translated from the Manipuri by
SOIBAM HARIPRIYA

We've been looking for long
at these incomplete images
reflected on this mirror in front of us
broken into fragments of shards,
We've been looking for long.
In one fragment my eye
in another my cheek
Likewise legs, hands, chest, neck –
everything is in pieces today,
these shadows on the pieces of the broken mirror.
Many centuries have passed thus
staring at this image cast back at us,
the two of us.
Yet never once did we murmur, anxiety
never felt, nor raised a question

asking, 'Why?'
You there stood as if a mountain
with proud shoulders, or
as if a bird flying about,
But I? You've tied me up
in a corner of this world
in front of this shattered mirror,
curbing my mobility,
forcing me to look
at my own distorted images.
Beholding these shadows, I dream
of my pubescent days –
challenging the others blooming,
how I had blossomed,
swaying to the rhythm of the breeze
under the veil
of the vast blue sky.
I had flowered in perfection, whole,
in front of this mirror
mesmerising the whole world.
As if repulsed by this sight,
As if dissatisfied
you had broken this mirror,
clutching a stone
with your very hands
at that very instance when you first stood by me.
Though for generations
it remained covered with a black veil,
barred by mountains,
an unstoppable storm churns today
from the thousands and thousands of hearts

of the images reflected in the shards of the broken mirror.
This rising storm is not in vain
it does not blow any other way, except yours.
This tempest is aimed towards you,
only towards you.

This poem was first published in Manipuri as 'Nongleise' in the collection of poems *Yenningtha Nangna Khongdoi Hullakpasida,* written by Moirangthem Borkanya, published in 2008 by Kulladwaja Konsam on behalf of Konsam Publications, Imphal. The book received the Manipur State Award for Literature in 2010.

As Spring Arrived

KSHETRIMAYUM SUBADANI

Translated from the Manipuri by
SAPAM SWEETIE

'When are you coming back?'

'I'm not sure. Why?'

'You usually don't return soon once you leave. Please don't do that this time too.'

'I can't help it. There's so much work at the office and it's all important. I can't just leave it and come.'

'Not everyone who's posted away from home acts like you. I feel uneasy staying alone in this isolated house with just the three children for company.'

'Didn't I ask Toyaima to look after your needs? He does come to help the children with their studies too sometimes, doesn't he? Why should you be afraid? I also come whenever I receive my salary.' He raised his voice slightly.

I knew that if I continued, he would hit me. So I said nothing. I was sad though. I had so much more to say, but he never paid much attention to my words, so there was no point even trying. I didn't want to start a fight when he was just leaving. What could one possibly do with the little money he handed over on his monthly visits? Was I not supposed to send my children to school? Even if I were to become a slave, I wanted my children to be successful.

Though I was still quite young, I started to sell the harvest from my kitchen garden in the market to earn a bit of money. Putting aside all shame and fear, thinking only of my children, I sat in the market with the middle-aged and old women, even though friends my age were still enjoying their youth. My elder daughter, a little more than a child herself, looked after her younger siblings in my absence. Occasionally, when I returned from the market, I would find Tada Toyaima with my children, helping them with their studies. Sometimes, on days when I brought home fish from the market, he would eat with us. He was from the same area, and close to the children's father as well. I thought of him as an elder brother, my Tada. Day and night, I dug the ground till my body ached, and I planted vegetables and watered them. When the afternoon sun cooled down a bit, I went to the market. It was a smaller market, one that opened only in the evenings. If I got late trying to sell off everything I had brought, I would get restless, worrying about my children. Though they have a father, it was as if he didn't exist.

One day, Iche Chaobi said to me at the market, 'Seems like Thoiba has taken a new wife in the hills where he's posted. I heard it's been a month since they've been living together in his quarters. Haven't you heard anything?'

87

I didn't reply. I wasn't the least bit surprised though. I knew how much my husband fooled around with women. With whom did he share his salary? why didn't he want to come home? why did he pick fights with me when he did return? why wouldn't he listen to me? I knew everything. Yet I endured all this and kept a tight control on myself.

Iche Chaobi continued, 'Go and stay with him for some time. Women should have a firm grasp on their men. Look for spells and amulets, consult shamans and astrologers. What can you do if you stay here just to sell a few things? Go and tear off that hussy's hair.'

I replied, 'Yes Iche, I'll go.'

'Go tomorrow.'

'Yes, I'll do that.'

'Does he think he can do whatever he wants? He should be taught a lesson', Iche Chaobi said angrily and left, fuming. She had said all these things because she cared for me.

I went to my husband the next morning. The woman wasn't there. But half of what I heard wasn't untrue. After scolding me as much as he could for visiting him, he stomped out. Exasperated, I stayed over at his place that night. He didn't come back. I sent people to look for him. But I didn't get to meet him, he was nowhere to be found. I came back the next day without waiting for him any further, worrying about how the children must be managing in my absence.

Tada Toyaima had looked after my children while I was away. He gave me the courage to be strong. But not long after, people began to talk in hushed voices. It soon reached my ears. I didn't like it. I didn't want to do anything wrong. So I told him, 'Tada, your visits have raised a lot of eyebrows, and human beings, as you know, have different perspectives. Your wife too must be anxious. I don't want to be the cause of any trouble.' He understood what I meant. He didn't reply, but left soon after. I didn't try to stop him either.

After that day, he didn't come by for a long time. But one day he suddenly resurfaced. It had been raining, and he was drenched when he entered. I was about to prepare dinner. Wiping his wet face with a handkerchief, he said, 'Ibemnungshi, I came in just for a while to get shelter from the rain. I won't be here long; I'll leave as soon as it stops raining.'

It was near impossible to wipe his soaked body with his little handkerchief. I gave him a dry cloth. I started a fire at the *phunga*, and asked him to sit there and dry himself. He seemed to have had a drink too. I didn't have the heart to ask him to leave in the rain either. The conversation began.

'Didn't Thoiba come by this month?'

'No, Tada.'

'Has he settled there with another woman?'

'I don't know.'

'It's going to be very difficult for you, what with the children too.'

'I must have been born at an inauspicious moment. So much hardship throughout my life!'

'Don't say such things, happier times will come too.'

'Tada, I don't believe my situation will improve…'

'Wait, Ibemnungshi,' he interrupted, 'do you hear that noise?'

'What? Oh yes, I hear it now.'

Soon, the din became louder. Not long after, I heard footsteps coming up the verandah. Someone knocked on the door, and called out, 'Ibemnungshi! Ibemnungshi! Open the door!'

As soon as I opened the door, a crowd thronged inside – the youths from the club and the Meira Paibi women. Noisily, they streamed into the kitchen. One of them shouted, 'Here! Here! The thief's here; we've caught the culprits. You hussy, fooling around with other men when your husband's not around! Come, let's shave her head and smear it with lime and turmeric.'

Someone replied, 'Don't let her go so easy. She shouldn't be allowed to live in this locality, banish her. Shave the man's head too. It's because of such immoral men and women that our locality's gone down so much.'

A woman suggested, 'Better marry them off right away, instead of shaving their heads.'

'Good, good, that's better', they all echoed, shouting and jostling. Toyaima too was shocked. It had been a long time since he had visited. And today he'd come in only to get shelter from the rain. And what was everyone doing now?

We pleaded, and tried to explain the real situation to the mob. But no one listened. They did not even pretend to listen. Quite blithely, they said, 'Do thieves ever own up to their crimes?'

In the night, they marched us off to the Pradhan's house, shouting all the while that they had caught the two thieves – the man and the woman. Paying no heed to our pleas, they forced us to go through the *keinya katpa*, a giving away of the bride ritual – making us garland each other with the mob as witnesses to the 'marriage', and then they declared us as man and wife.

What would we do now? Lightning had struck without even rainclouds looming. Where would we go now? The mob made that decision too, 'Go and stay at Toyaima's house.'

Should I cry or laugh? How should I appeal when my mouth and tongue has been cut off? They herded us towards Tada Toyaima's house. I finally found my voice when the crowd dispersed at the gate, 'Tada, I'll go back now.'

'I'll walk you home, Ibemma.'

'It's all right. I can go alone.'

'They've all left, you won't meet them. But how can you go alone in this darkness?'

'Who should I be scared of now at this time when life or death itself doesn't matter?'

I reached my house. The children were sitting by the *phunga* with Iche Chaobi. She glared at me. But she was the only one who knew me. Though I've never been one to cry easily, tears streamed down my face endlessly that night. I wept to my heart's content. What could be more humiliating and dishonourable than this?

When he heard the news, he came. Without hearing me out, overcome by his fury, he thrashed me like an animal and chased me out of the house. I had thought of letting my husband kill me, but he didn't. He dragged me by my hair out to the streets. What should I do? Where should I go? I found no refuge at my parents' home or with my relatives either. The news spread like wildfire. Left without any options, I stayed at a hotel. A few days passed. I had no money to buy food or pay the hotel rent. Is it not human behaviour to sympathise with the sufferings of others? Yes, this was what I believed. I narrated my story to the hotel owner. He listened attentively and offered to help. I was elated, thinking kind-hearted people still existed. But it wasn't for long. All my trust was shattered soon after.

One night, there was a knock at the door. I opened it, thinking it must be the kind hotel owner. That night I lost my honour for the first time. And then they gave me some money to keep my mouth shut.

I had money now but what would I do with it? I made the decision – I would earn money. The world revolves around money. I soon had trading money in my hands. I came out of the hotel. I rented another place. I started selling assorted items. Gradually, I began to make a profit. With this, I set up a small shop. But for whom was I amassing money? It's when I ponder upon this question that my tears find freedom. But my heart says stoically, 'Such is life.'

It has been ten years since the incident. The dark blot on my honour has faded away slowly. How my husband fooled around in the hills for years in the past, leaving me alone with my children in that isolated house, and how he came to know the truth gradually, how this realisation had taken many years, and how he had only come to regret this now – all this information wasn't new to my ears; it came to be told and retold over and over again. 'Thoiba is suffering; he has come to his senses. Your children have never forgotten you.' It was the mention of my children that made my heart ache anew. I ask myself again – for whom have I earned so much? The messages came steadily, asking me to return. But why should I go back on my own? I am also human.

One day, quite unexpectedly, Spring arrived. His words reached my ears, 'Ibemnungshi, I've come to take you home.'

This short story was first published in Manipuri as 'Yeningthana Lakpada' in the collection of short stories *Yeningthana Lakpada*, written by Kshetrimayum Subadabi, published in 2000 by Khomdram Dorendra on behalf of Linthoingambi Publications, Imphal.

The Detour

BIMABATI THIYAM ONGBI

Translated from the Manipuri by
SONIA WAHENGBAM

The heart of Khwairamband Keithel! I was flanked by market stalls on all sides. The fumes from the huge soot-laden fires of the big oil lamps will definitely stain my body, and my clothes. And this evening crowd! My nose starts itching. The desire to buy fish wanes.

Some three or four stalls away from where I stand, a youngish-looking woman, her head hung low, sprinkles some water on the fish lying on the upturned cover of the tin container. She turns them over every now and again. I walk up to her and ask, 'How much for the two *rohu* fish?'

Maybe she hasn't heard me, she doesn't respond. Raising my voice a bit, I ask again, 'Hey! How much are these two *rohu* of yours?'

Stroking the fish, she replies, 'They're a hundred and eighty per kilo. You can have them for a hundred and fifty rupees.' This without raising her head.

'That's too much. The two fish aren't even the same size. I'll pay a hundred and forty.'

'Best you look elsewhere then. I can't give them to you at that price.' She looks up as she speaks.

'Eh!' I exclaim, taken aback at the sight of the face now visible in the flickering light of the lamp. She too seems shocked. Recognition dawns in both our eyes.

'Sanatombi!'

She doesn't reply. Her hand remains suspended mid-stroke. After a while, she slowly drops her hand and lowers her eyes. And softly she says, 'Pass me your bag, I'll put in the fish.'

As Sanatombi puts the fish inside the bag, I drop a couple of one-hundred-rupee notes. Silently, she hands the bag back to me. As I turn to leave, she calls out, 'Wait! I haven't given you the change.'

'Keep it.'

'Hmm, but that's not done. Taking more than what's due of another's money isn't right.'

'Another's money' – her words instantly strike at my heart. Pain rises deep within. I take the remaining money from her and leave without saying a word.

In the past too, when she used to be close to me, Sanatombi never accepted favours from others. She would often say, 'I don't want help from anyone. I don't want to eat for free with another's money. I am also a human being; I'll work with my strength, toil hard. At the very least, I won't starve.' Her every word used to make me think. When she and I were together, life seemed to have a meaning. How astonishing destiny is! Sometimes it becomes our worst enemy – this I had come to realise when she and I parted ways. 'My family doesn't like you' – these few words had made her drift away from me. In truth, hers was a small family – mother, younger brother and Sanatombi. Quite different from my own family. But I had never thought, not for even a moment, that this very issue would drive her away from me.

The next day, I could not concentrate on my office work, wanting to wind up swiftly. By the time the clock struck four in the evening, almost everyone had left for the day. Despite my desire to leave early, I had to stay on late to complete something. Finally, when the work is done, I take out my two-wheeler and start driving in the direction of my thoughts.

Two men are standing in front of her stall, bargaining. Today too, Sanatombi sits with her face lowered. I stand to one side and watch. I don't like the look in the eyes of one of the men, or the manner in which he is speaking. Sanatombi silently strokes the fish inside her tin container, turning them up and down. One of the men says, 'Allow me to give a hundred and fifty rupees for the two fish. Please don't refuse. A beauty like you shouldn't price things so high. Please, take pity on us and say yes, won't you?'

At the man's words, Sanatombi raises her head and shoots him a sharp look. 'Leave, let's not prolong this discussion. You're wasting my time. Go, let me make my sales.' She quickly covers the fish with a cloth. Taken aback at the tone of her voice, the two men stand, nonplussed, for a while and then walk away without any further words.

As they depart, Sanatombi releases a long breath and rapidly scans the thronging shoppers around her. She catches sight of me. She doesn't raise her eyes again.

I go up to her stall and call softly, 'Sanatombi.'

She doesn't reply. Never once had I thought that she would become a market vendor, sitting thus in the market and selling fish. The urge to know more comes upon me. I step in closer, and ask, 'Sanatombi, are you upset with my visit?'

She remains silent, but lowers her head further. I continue, 'I'm still finding it hard to believe that you are here in this condition.'

'Umm', she mumbles.

'Isn't it late? Don't you have to get back?'

'I'll leave once I sell everything here. If I don't manage, by tomorrow this farm fish will spoil.'

'You're right. But if you wait to sell all that fish, it will get quite late. Isn't he coming to pick you up?'

Again, no answer. Her silence disturbs me. 'Have I said something I shouldn't have?' I ask myself.

And then, to her, 'Sanatombi, did I say something wrong?'

'Nothing wrong, Taichou. But you probably don't know that it's been more than two years since he passed away … nearly three now.'

This time it is my turn for silence. I'm at a loss for words. But my disobedient eyes remain staring at her.

'How much for these two fish?' A woman comes up to ask.

'A hundred and sixty rupees.'

'I'll pay a hundred and forty.'

'That's not even my cost price, give a hundred and fifty-five.'

'Okay then, take a hundred and fifty.'

'It's getting so late … very well, I'll give these to you. Here, take them.'

The woman leaves, happy with the bargain. A mixture of small catfish and mudfish remains on the upturned cover of the tin container.

'Sanatombi, I'll buy all this remaining fish. How much should I pay?'

'Taichou, you can just take it.'

'No, no, that can't be. Here, take a hundred rupees. It's quite a lot of fish.'

'Taichou, I don't want anything extra.'

'It's me who's giving you the money, not a stranger.'

'To me, Taichou, you too are a stranger.'

Ish! Shame washes all over me at her words. She continues calmly, 'From the time he died till now, I've never taken any help from others. I am also human. As long as I can, I want to earn with my own strength and labour, and thus bring up my children. Taichou, the eldest one is old enough now. She's able to help with some of the household work. She also looks after her younger brother in my absence.'

'How many kids?'

'Only two. The youngest one is also old enough to be left at home.'

She deducts eighty rupees from the hundred I dropped on her fish container and returns twenty to me.

'Taichou, please take this.'

'Keep it. Buy some snacks for your children.'

'It's okay, Taichou. Every day I take home something for them. I'll buy some snacks today too.' She was adamant.

'Sanatombi, do you blame me?' Taking a long breath, I ask, my voice trembling a bit. Is this a question from my rebellious heart?

She doesn't reply, but just sits there, staring up at me. I can't understand the meaning of her gaze, nor can I meet her eyes. And there are so many people around, I can't muster up the courage to repeat my question for fear they may hear.

She speaks after a while. 'Taichou, he was a kind-hearted man, always putting me and the kids first. For our sakes, he didn't rest even for a moment. That day he had gone to the market with our son. He saw that a car was about to hit the child, and he ran and pushed him away but got hit himself. Our son survived, but he did not.'

She doesn't answer my question but tells me this story as she gathers her things together. I don't know how to respond. 'What after that?' I ask.

'After that I've been trying to raise my kids without taking favours from anyone.'

'Oi, Sanatombi! Wrap up, let's go', another woman vendor shouts from a distance.

'Iche, I'm done. You gather up your things too.'

She turns to me and says, 'Taichou, I'll be going then.'

'The transportation's bad in your area. How're you going back?'

'There are many auto-rickshaws that go to our area.'

'Okay then. Go, it's quite late.'

I watch as she hauls up the tin container on top of her head and walks away. What else could I do? I also head straight home without buying anything else.

That night, after learning of her husband's death, I can't sleep thinking of her, I toss and turn in my bed. My wife asks, 'Can't you sleep? Is anything wrong? Are you unwell?'

'No, I'm fine', I reply. I can't let her – she who thinks about me all the time – know about my inner turmoil. But inside my mind, I have many questions for Sanatombi.

'Sanatombi, how did your situation come to this? I want to help you as much as I can. Don't go out to the market … If he were still here, you wouldn't be struggling like this…' This way and that, there are layers and layers of the unending questions.

Today's a Sunday. Since the office is closed, I think of visiting her again. But it's early, and I can't bring myself to take a step forward. Impatient, I wait for the evening to arrive. For some unknown reason, my heart is beating faster than usual today. A strange anxiety seems to have overtaken me.

The fish-vending area in the market is thronging with shoppers. Chaotic and claustrophobic, it is quite difficult to walk up to her stall.

Isn't this her spot? Yes, it is. It was only yesterday that I saw her here. Yes, this is her place. I look around again. I never thought she might not be here, in her vending stall.

An old woman selling an assortment of catfish and mudfish nearby is watching me keenly. She asks, 'Ibungo, aren't you the one who came yesterday?'

'Yes, I am.'

'Sanatombi left early today. She asked me to pass on a message to you.'

'What did she say?'

'She said she wants to earn for her children. She also asked you not to visit her again.'

What could I say? I could no longer stand there and face the old woman. An especially frisky catfish leapt out of the old woman's tin container. Slashing my foot with the sharp spine on its fin, it landed on the ground and soon wiggled its way out of sight into the nearby drain.

This short story was first published in Manipuri as 'Eetheikhraba Eechel' in the collection of short stories *Eetheikhraba Eechel*, written by Bimabati Thiyam Ongbi, published in 2013 by Sarda Translations & Publishing Group, Manipur.

Woman

KOIJAM SANTIBALA

Translated from the Manipuri by
AKOIJAM SUNITA

In the quiet of the night
Under the seductive dance of the moonlight
Accompanied by a sweet fragrance like the *thaballei* flowers
My dishevelled hair
Spread wide across my back
When I came to you
You said –
'You are an enchantress
A goddess of the night,
I worship you in my heart.'

I laughed silently
What do you know!
It is only the fragrance of the *thaballei* that you desire
It is only the moonlight that pleases you.

Even if for a day,
Have you sat beneath the *thaballei* vines, for her
Spent a whole night there?
Within the folds of your deep sleep
It is only her, who quietly
Spreads her fragrance around;
But again
She is branded a wanton woman,
With a roving eye
Weaving entrapments of desire.

When morning comes, the *thaballei* flowers
Lose their fragrance.
The lamp of life too will be extinguished.
She will cry with the *singgarei* flowers
Rolling in agony on the ground.
You didn't shed a tear ever
When the *singgarei* fell, scattering widely
When the *thaballei* fragrance concealed itself.

And yet you say,
You worship her in your heart.
I cry,
For the bewitching of many hearts
In the quiet night like the *thaballei* flowers;
For receiving the title, 'Goddess'.

What has the *thaballei* ever desired?
Its fragrance alone
Is her prized possession.
Therefore,

I will cry furthermore
Till this night comes to an end
Till a morning takes away
This final heartache.

This poem was first published in Manipuri as 'Nupi' in the collection of poems *Pallon Wangma*, written by Koijam Santibala, published in 2013, by RK Sanayaima Devi for The Cultural Forum, Manipur.

The Crimson Tide

NEPRAM MAYA

Translated from the Manipuri by
PAONAM THOIBI

Tondonbi stopped rowing in the middle of the lake, hauling up the oars onto her small boat. Silently, she sat there, seemingly oblivious to the vast expanse of water. The sight of the small huts built atop the scattered and isolated *phumdi* floating on the greenish waters reminded her of events intertwined with her past life, making her heart cry again and again. She stared intently at how the limitless blue sky and the vast greenish lake merged to become one. But where is it that they actually joined together? No, they did not. They didn't meet at all. It was just the illusion of a union.

Likewise, the beginning and the end of Tondonbi's life too cannot be woven together – just as those hearts which believed in forcible unions will not be able to connect with the simple rural life of people content with the little they have; just as the heart devoid of the slightest drop of pity will not be able to come closer to the love-filled hearts of the common people. Tondonbi frequently denounced the heart that believed in this seeming union between the vast sky and the limitless stretch of water.

It is only for a few moments that the sight of the crimson and orange evening clouds, their reflection spreading across the surface of the lake and the reddish hue it all lends to the water, mesmerizes the heart. Tondonbi could, however, never forget the bloodied waves that rose with each swelling tide on the greenish lake that day. For a long time she had kept a hold on the uncontrollable rush of emotions that surged up in her heart. She had even stopped rowing her boat towards this place, promising herself that she wouldn't fish here even if poverty threatened to bring her to the brink of death. How had she found herself rowing in this direction today? Like one who has lost her bearings, she sat there, silent and unmoving, in the middle of the lake as the boat went adrift, floating freely in whichever direction the wind took her. She woke up from her reverie only when the tip of her boat struck against the floating *phumdi*.

Slowly she climbed out of her boat and onto the *phumdi*. Like the rippling water striking at the *phumdi* and then rolling back again into a series of waves, a turbulence rose in Tondonbi's heart at the unceasing upsurge of memories. Pain shot through her. Her present merged again with that part of her past life that was entangled with this isolated and seemingly uninhabited place. Her legs and arms became numb, and she went into a waking nightmare...

'How are you managing to sleep? The blanket is all twisted and bunched up on one side. What luck I have ... sleeping together with a person who makes a house with his knees in this cold weather!'

She twisted and turned restlessly. The makeshift bamboo frame serving as their bed creaked as she moved. Paying no heed to her complaints, Tomchou asked, 'Tondonbi, do you have a *biri* stashed aside by any chance?'

'There's a butt somewhere. No fresh stick.'

'Let me have a puff. It's so cold.'

Noisily, he took a hard, long drag and blew out the smoke. Then he threw away the stub on the floor by the bed.

After a while, Tondonbi murmured, 'Tomorrow they'll come. The scheduled days they marked are over now. They'll ask us to leave.'

'Why should we go? Just because they say so? Death is inevitable. This life too is like being dead. These are times when everyone does as they wish and talks to whomever they wish. We'll see now whether they survive or I die.'

'Good grief! No way! All will be lost! Don't you go up against them. Let them stay here. Please don't confront these brutes.'

'Those rascals! Just because they have power in their hands! Just think, when we had nothing and were struggling so hard, never once did they ask what we needed, how they can help us. And now, they say they stand for the people, for the land, do you even believe that?'

'Even if I don't, does anyone dare to say anything? That's why I'm telling you not to confront them.'

'Tondonbi, maybe it's better that we don't even exist.'

Tondonbi didn't respond. Silently, she recalled how hard they had struggled to build their hut atop the *phumdi* on Loktak lake without any thought for whether they had food to eat or not. What hopes they had nurtured then, their skinny bodies apparently impervious to exhaustion! How they had ferried bamboo and other construction materials back and forth in their small boat, undeterred by the rain or the sun. They had tried to make it just about livable and yet strong enough to withstand the winds, knotting the bamboo together with ropes and thin bamboo strips.

And today these people come, using their clout to oust them – is this even humane? Tondonbi loathes the idea but also fears what they might do if she openly voices her resentment. Those who fear have a long life and those who don't have no inkling of what might befall them today or tomorrow. It's because of this fear that no one has been able to speak out, why they pretend to sympathize, why their hands and feet remain tied with power and their mouths gagged with fear. The price of a human being too is decided after death. Humans have become heartless. They seem to have forgotten that it is much easier to conquer the hearts of people with words coming from a sincere heart, instead of trying to dominate through power. In their greed, they have become unable to trust one another.

Overwhelmed by her emotions, Tondonbi cried out, 'No one bothered to even inquire about us during our hard times. Now when we've used up all our strength and managed to have a home, they're trying to snatch it away from us.'

'Who're you talking to? Have you gone back to sleep?'

'No, I can't sleep. I was thinking whether we are really leaving just because they want us to. When we have struggled so much to build this hut…'

'What if we don't go? And if we do, where will we go?'

Tondonbi fell silent once again. With each of her husband's incomplete sentences, her heart became more troubled. How hard those shrivelled arms had struggled to keep the loaded boat straight on the water – the weight bringing the boat almost at level with the water surface of Loktak Lake. How the sweat falling from the near-deadened body, dead-tired from cutting through the *phumdi*, had merged into the lake. This was how they had built the hut. Tondonbi recalled their struggles…

'Tondombi, today I have fastened the *phumdi* down with some rocks and bamboo. It won't move now, or be swept away by the wind. Pemma, my dear, when this is complete we won't have to take shelter in someone else's home. We'll finally have a stable home of our own. We'll be able to live now! Tomorrow, let's try to bring some of the dry *kambong* leaves to make the thatch.'

Smiling, he continued, 'Tondonbi, if our beloved mother, the Lady Loktak hadn't existed, poor people like us couldn't have survived. Because of her, our sufferings have been lifted to some extent.'

Tomchou's fervent aspiration was that he himself shouldn't let life defeat him. Life should sail in the direction one wishes. Defeat or victory rests in one's efforts. Never once did he think of surrendering his struggles in life. Tomchou struggled, challenging life, desiring to win in the battle of life, to gain the fruit of his labour. He thatched and walled the hut with the dried *kambong* leaves. From the moment they started living in their small hut, despite being so poor, he was able to realise the real meaning of life. Many desires which had hitherto been dormant in his heart were awakened anew. The chilly winter mornings, when the bluish-green lake is covered in fog, and one can hardly see the next person; the distant strands of *khullang eshei*, the workers' song that stirred the heart; the moment when he returned cheerfully with the fish he had caught; the way his naive heart would burst tunefully into song regardless of whether it was timely or not – Tondonbi's heart could not forget all these. She recalls everything.

'Oh my! Do you even know what song you are singing? With your looks? Aren't you afraid that passersby will make fun of you?'

'Pemma, can't I even sing a song with joy? If I sing, it's none of their business. I'll sing. Let them say what they want, I'll sing to my heart's content.'

And he sings, '*Sabi Ine macha Pamubi nangbu tarabra … lemlei ngabu talluba…*'[1]

'Why you! Stop, stop, enough … please stop…!' Their laughter still lingers to this day. At that moment when they had laughed so joyfully, there had been no trace of fear in their hearts. There was only contentment. But it was also at this very moment – when they had thought they would live on with many happy memories – that the unbelievable moment had arrived. The big words that came out of those small mouths were deeply offensive. As Tondonbi and her husband rowed away from the hut, she had wished that those men would drown in the lake that very instant. The couple had faced so many difficulties, and now, today in the middle of the water, they had to endure this. Silently, they sat in the boat. Without any respect towards the couple who could well be their parents, the intruders had spoken

---

[1] In this song, the fisherman recounts a fishing trip to his beloved.

thus because of the power they wielded. What kind of independence was this that they were demanding? Which righteous path did they want to tread? Tondonbi had been livid at their insolence.

Suddenly, she spoke out loud, 'Will their parents even grieve when they are gone?'

'Whom are you talking about, huh…? Did you forget that we are in the middle of the lake? Do you want me to drown you? She doesn't even think before she speaks!'

Tondonbi was taken aback at the fury of her husband's words. Her heart sank. Lowering her voice a bit, she said, 'If we had worked together, they would have known the price of our sweat. They hold power in their hands. Even though we hold them up on our shoulders as they try to achieve their goals, they treat us so badly that we're unable to even pull up our legs.'

Tomchou didn't reply. In the darkness of the waning moon, they rowed on, listlessly. Slowly, the boat floated down the lake. As they reached the shore, someone suddenly grasped the tip of their boat and jerked it closer. A hand seized her husband by his shoulder and dragged him off the boat. The small boat rocked wildly. Tondonbi held on, shocked. Suddenly she heard her husband being beaten up.

'Tell us where they got off. What were you guys carrying back and forth? Guns? Or food supplies for them? Go on, take us there…'

She didn't hear her husband reply. Except for his yelps of pain and the sound of their hard blows landing on him, she didn't hear anything else. When Tondonbi pleaded, 'Please don't hit him. We are innocent', the voice that shouted back at her was extremely unpleasant.

'Even in your old age, how much money do you want to earn, huh? Lead us to them or else we will kill you, do you understand?!'

In the dim moonlight, they took her husband away in his own boat. Some more men dressed in fatigues followed in other boats. Tondonbi stood there, looking at the receding figures, crying her heart out.

When she thought of what that withered, weather-beaten body, moulded by a life filled with struggle, must have endured, Tondonbi didn't know what to do. She could not bear it any longer.

When day broke, the lake was cordoned off. No one was allowed to enter or leave. The path of many who entered the lake to search for fish was cut off. The surrounding area was heavily guarded by armed personnel in uniform. The criteria of 'disclosure' or 'non-disclosure' now rested solely on Tomchou. Both sides did not know the hearts of human beings, nor did they want to know. Tondonbi's heart was overwhelmed with resentment. Her pent-up sorrow made her sit up like a madwoman. Where would she go, with whom could she plead for her husband? Time, on the other hand, crept on.

After they took him away along with many harsh and fearful words, she didn't get to see Tomchou alive again. In that dark night, they ended her husband's life. Driven away from the hut on the *phumdi* under whose shadow they had sought refuge, did they want both husband and wife to drown in the waters? Because of them, he was gone, forever gone. He had led the soldiers the wrong way, deliberately misleading them. It was for those who had driven the two of them away so mercilessly, for their sake that he had given up his life. But what have they ever done for the poverty-ridden common people?

The crimson and orange clouds of the approaching dusk spread out in all directions. The bluish-green waters of Loktak lake too changed in colour, assuming a monstrous and fiery red hue. There he lay peacefully in his own boat, seemingly in a deep slumber, clad only in his *loukhao* shirt and *khudei* loincloth, both dyed red in his own blood. His oar, which had always accompanied him like a walking stick, lay there smeared with his blood. Tondonbi stared on, transfixed. Her unfocussed eyes couldn't see her husband even though he lay there before her. Her thoughts raced. To the two groups, who do not know the distinction between right and wrong, and instead gifted death to the common people caught in between, she wanted to ask, 'What is his fault?'

Their small hut which they had built with much hardship, without knowing food or sleep, these people had left as a heap of ashes on the *phumdi*. This hut that they had built merging the sweat from their body with the water of the lake became the sole reason for his red blood to again flow into the waters of Loktak. Who is at fault – Tondonbi and her husband for searching for a way to end their penury, or was it the mighty and the powerful who flex their muscles?

Tondonbi sat motionless on the *phumdi*. The sun too gradually retreated towards the hillocks. The reddish waves slowly swelled up in the green lake. The faint strains of the *khullang eshei* that her husband once used to sing so lovingly reached her ears. Tondonbi looked on unblinking at the crimson tide forming up on the lake.

This short story was first published in Manipuri as 'Ngangleinaba Eethak Eepom' in the collection of short stories *Ngangleinaba Eethak Eepom*, written by Nepram Maya, published in 2010 and 2015 by Nepram Shanti Devi for The Cultural Forum, Manipur.

My Children's Photographs

NINGOMBAM SATYABATI

Translated from the Manipuri by
SAPAM SWEETIE

'Mama, when I grow up, will I fly an aeroplane?'

'Why of course you will, my child!'

'When I become a big man, my photo will get published in the newspaper, right Mama?'

'Of course, my son!'

'Mama, what will Cheche be when she grows up?'

'Your sister's a girl. She'll get married and be taken away to someone else's house.'

'*Mey*! No! I'll not let them take her. I'll seat her on my aeroplane and fly her to America, and let her stay there instead. Then she won't have to marry.'

'Crazy child! Do you love your sister?'

'Yes, I do.'

'How much?'

'This much!' He gestures, arching his little hands towards his back.

'Who do you love the most among the three of us – Baba, Mama or Cheche?'

'I love all three of you.'

'Ha! You kids nowadays! So young, yet the things you utter with your little mouths!'

Both parents were crazy about Momocha's endless questions, they found them endearing. They thought, 'This must be it … the cord that binds everyone firmly in the marital life of a man and woman all over the world – the love for one's child.'

Today, their daughter will participate in a painting competition being conducted by an organization in Imphal. She will represent her school. Momocha's going too. After an early lunch, their mother dresses them and leads them to pray at the household deity, *Sanamahi*, placed inside the house. Then they bow at the foot of the tulsi plant in the centre of the courtyard.

'Paint well, my child.

'Yes, Ima.'

'Today, we'll take Momocha to Khwairamband market', says the father.

'Please buy him a nice shirt, Father.'

'Why yes, I'll surely buy one for my son!'

'For Cheche too.'

'Of course!'

'For Mama too.'

'Yes, yes.'

'Mama, bye-bye.'

She stands at the gate and watches as long as she can as the children wave their small hands and walk off, leading their father away briskly.

The sun has set. Darkness has descended. Just going to and fro to the gate, arching to see if her husband and children have returned, has left Momo-Ma's eyes utterly exhausted. 'Where could they possibly be? What is holding them up … he never knows when to return once he leaves', she berates her husband. Lighting the oil lantern, she sits down by the gate, straining her eyes, waiting for their return.

Passers-by and acquaintances ask sympathetically, 'Momo-Ma, what are you doing there?'

'Whom are you waiting for, Ibemma?'

In the darkness, the weaver who had gone to sell her fabrics to the market vendors rushes down the road, clutching her yarn box tightly. Visibly terrified, she tells her, as she hurries by, 'Ibemsa, shooting at Khwairamband! I'm lucky I'm not hurt or dead. There's no way buses can come through. I've been able to get away only by the grace of God. This is my good fortune. It's a bizarre time, it's war. If a bomb explodes in such a crowded market, people are bound to die. Everyone at home must be distressed.' And she walks on quickly. Momo-Ma is left completely dumbstruck.

Neighbours and relatives try to console her, to allay her mounting fear.

'With vehicles not plying, both the father and the children must be held up somewhere.'

'Imaipemma, they'll be here before dawn. After all, Imphal is not far!'

'Have your dinner and go sleep well, daughter-in-law.'

The neighbours help Momo-Ma up and escort her inside the house.

It's early morning. How have the newspapers managed to arrive? 'Dead, dead, confirmed, confirmed,' the newspapers scream. Everyone begins to ask about Momo-Ma. The entire locality launches a search. Some jump into the ponds, some climb the granaries, some scour corners and open fields, and some look in the thickets.

Three or four men hold Momo-Ma by the arms and drag her in. Her hair has come undone, the tight knot now slack, thick masses of hair cascading down her back. Her upper cloth is loose and they can't unclench her hands. Someone says, 'She was snatching newspapers from people in the market.'

'What'll become of her if she goes crazy and starts roaming the streets?'

'Hi-hi-hi!' Momo-Ma laughs hysterically. She looks at the crumpled newspaper and then holds it to her breast. Then she raises it to her lips and begins to kiss it, exclaiming happily, '*Ahai yo*! *Tash*! Today my children's photographs are in the newspapers!'

Written in March 1992, this short story was first published in Manipuri as 'Ichagi Photo' in the collection of short stories *Amaangba Nonglakki Nongthang*, written by Satyabati Ningombam, published in 2000 by Ningombam Ranjan and Samananda for Manipur Sahitya Parishad, Thoubal Branch, Manipur.

Torch Warriors

Toijam Sarojini Chanu

Translated from the Manipuri by
Thingnam Anjulika Samom

Coiling up their hair into buns at the back of their heads
Tightening their *khwangchet*, the sash around their waist
Picking up a flaming torch in hand
Emerge battalions of the torch warriors.

They walk through the late night
Unsleeping, even for a wink
No, it isn't atop the Baruni Hills
No, it isn't at the Shiva temple there.

Warring ceaselessly
Against the intoxicated masses
In darkened restaurant cabins of the city
In dense lanes of the village.

No, it isn't to raise the victory flag
Atop Himalayan peaks
No, it isn't to raise cries of victory
In the battlefields of the world.

It's only because of the desire
To hold in their embrace
A living child of their own.

This poem was first published in Manipuri as 'Meira Lanmi' in the collection of poems *Lan Khammu Ima*, written by Toijam Sarojini, published in 2006 by Hawaibam ongbi Pakpi Devi on behalf of Iramdam Meeyamgi Apunba Khorjeilup (IMAKHOL), Manipur.

Don't Wait

TOIJAM SAROJINI CHANU

Translated from the Manipuri by
THINGNAM ANJULIKA SAMOM

Birthed for the motherland
You came to this land;
Growing up in its soil
Your wings now have spread.

Now roam here
Huge, hairy tigers.
They hide their venomous paws
Behind you.

With the power you gave, they've
Eliminated many lives
With those claws stretching out
From behind you.

How many Sanamacha,[1]
How many Bijoykumar,
Have you taken away secretly
From their mother's laps?

How many Manorama
Have you preyed on?
What number was Jamkholet
That you had secretly buried?

Reverend Ashuli,
You skinned alive.
How impregnable
Is your strength, your power!

At the outskirts of the towns
At the foot of hill ranges
The huge tigers roam freely
Wrapped within the folds of your power.

Indelible from memory even today
The hill flower Chanu Rose
Trampled at first bloom
By the dutiful Major himself.

---

[1] Sanamacha, Bijoykumar, Manorama, Jamkholet, Reverend Ashuli, Chanu Rose and Sangita are among many who were tortured, raped, had disappeared after arrest by the army, or lost their lives at the hands of the army during counter-insurgency operations in Manipur.

This rare human life
That even Lord Brahma himself is said to envy,
But why did you take your own life
Oh, innocent Sangita?

For many years
Having been with you,
Today I am fed up
Repulsed by your sight.

Disgusted by you,
Without food and drink
For many years now, she stays
Meitei lass Sharmila.[2]

Unwilling to see you,
Setting himself on fire
Extinguished his own life
Meitei youth Chittaranjan.[3]

Twelve Meitei Leima, those aged married women
Stripped and displayed all which remains concealed.
No, it isn't our tradition,
It was because of loathing for you.

---

[2] Irom Chanu Sharmila who fasted for 16 years demanding repeal of Armed Forces Special Powers Act (AFSPA), 1958

[3] Pebam Chittaranjan who immolated himself and died as a result while protesting against Armed Forces Special Powers Act (AFSPA), 1958

Therefore go, you go away
AFSPA,[4] you go away
Don't wait for the Meitei women
To kill themselves, jumping into the sacrificial fire.

In every Kanglei house,
Every young Kanglei male
To take up swords in hand
Don't wait, you do not wait.

This poem was first published in Manipuri as 'Ngairanu' in the collection of poems *Lan Khammu Ima*, written by Toijam Sarojini, published in 2006 by Hawaibam ongbi Pakpi Devi on behalf of Iramdam Meeyamgi Apunba Khorjeilup (IMAKHOL), Manipur.

---

[4] Armed Forces Special Powers Act (AFSPA) 1958.

Voices from the Womb

RK Sanahanbi (Likkhombi) Chanu

Translated from the Manipuri by
PAONAM THOIBI

The unborn children inside the womb
To their beloved mothers, ask
Mother!
Are there still sit-in-protests
On the big streets?

Yes, yes, my daughter, they're protesting.

Mother!
Are there still torch rallies
During the nights?

Yes, yes, my son, they're still rallying.

What about setting fire to effigies?

Yes, yes, they're busy burning them down.

Then, Mother,
Bombs, guns and mock bombs,
Tear gas, rubber bullets
Are they still aplenty and unrestrained?

Yes, they are in plenty
Because this is a free land.

Then dear Mother,
Let us stay in your womb forever.

Hah!

This poem was first published in Manipuri as 'Siyomnungda Sum Leijarage' in the collection *Pibiro Ima Natambak Ama*, written by RK Sanahanbi (Likkhombi) Chanu, published in 2015 by Sanaton Rajkumar for the Iramdam Meeyamgi Apunba Khorjei Lup (Imakhol), Manipur.

I Too Am A Soldier

RK Sanahanbi (Likkhombi) Chanu

Translated from the Manipuri by
PAONAM THOIBI

Even if my eyes are blind
Even if my ears are deaf
I see and hear all
Through my heart
Through my mind
Because I too have a soul,
Because I too am alive!

Even if my mouth is shut
Regrets there are many
Love, passion, desires,
Hunger and thirst,
Just like you I crave;
Because I too have a heart,
Because I too am human.

But
Since you who should see, decided not to see
Since you who should know, decided not to know
I chose not to grieve.
I too am a soldier just like you
Sent forth to fight
In this battlefield called life.

This poem was first published in Manipuri as 'Lanmini Eisu' in the collection of poems *Pibiro Ima Natambak Ama*, written by RK Sanahanbi (Likkhombi) Chanu, published in 2015 by Sanaton Rajkumar for the Iramdam Meeyamgi Apunba Khorjei Lup (Imakhol), Manipur.

At the Morgue

MUFIDUN NISHA

Translated from the Manipuri by
SHREEMA NINGOMBAM

For the news
Of her child taken forcibly away
At gunpoint
Now untraceable, without any clues
Sitting at the morgue, awaits
The poor mother.

Of those taken away beyond the gate
Of those concealed, disappeared,
The destination is the morgue.

(They) will come without fail
To rest at the morgue
To sign in for the final time

To hear the laments
Of mothers, fathers, and siblings.

This poem was first published in Manipuri as 'Morgue Ta' in the collection of poems *Mingshel da Leichil*, written by Mufidun Nisha, published in 2006 by the author for the Writers Union, Manipur.

The Reply

MUFIDUN NISHA

Translated from the Manipuri by
SHREEMA NINGOMBAM

The pregnant woman asked repeatedly
When can I deliver?
Hasn't the time come?

The midwife replied,
Hold on … even though you are tired,
O pregnant woman.
The moment you deliver,
Yet another tragedy
Will surely befall you.

Asked again fearfully
The pregnant woman
Whose hours have arrived,
When can I open my eyes?
When will my pains cease?

The midwife replied
When your agony is gone
Another major illness
Might again afflict you
So bear it even if painful, close your eyes tight
Like your enduring self.

This poem was first published in Manipuri as 'Wahangdugi Paokhum' in the anthology *Mingshel da Leichil*, written by Mufidun Nisha, published in 2006 by the author for the Writers Union, Manipur.

Sati Interview

NINGOMBAM SANATOMBI

Translated from the Manipuri by
KUNDO YUMNAM

Oh dear! What do I do? Would I have the guts to climb up the stage at this age? All the eminent women of the land must be gathered there. Had it been about pots and pans, or brooms and mops, I could have been quite the orator.

'Ima, what are you murmuring about?' my daughter interrupted.

'Hei! Stop chattering and just finish your chores. And fix dinner with your father when he returns. I'm tied up with some important work.'

'What important work?'

'The day after tomorrow is International Women's Day. I'll be presenting a seminar paper.'

Mapa Ibungo walks in as we speak. Father and daughter murmur something and they chuckle. Surely it's something about me.

I take out a pen and a sheet of paper. Where shall I start? Nope! I can't be hasty with this. I should arrange my thoughts first about what to write.

'Ima, should I prepare *iromba* or a stew?'

'You are such a bother, dear. *Iromba* or stew, you decide!'

The first line of my paper in my head, and now it's gone! I close my eyes and try to concentrate. Ah! There it is! I'll start like this.

'What's the topic you are going to speak on?' he asks.

'Women's Rights in Hindu Mythology.'

The sentences that I had painstakingly constructed vanish again. This father-daughter duo can be really annoying. I try to recollect the lines, but in vain. Should I just write down the conclusion first?

'Ima, let's eat.'

I put my pen down on the empty sheet of paper.

After dinner I return to my spot. I try to recall my thoughts.

'It's going to be quite entertaining, Panthoi! Your kitchen-bound mother is trying to go after women's rights.'

Mapa Ibungo's words hurt a little.

'Don't! If all those who are kitchen-bound start to shout out for their rights from every kitchen, the land will be drowned in their clamour.'

'Ima, can you still spell your name correctly? Hope you don't embarrass yourself.' The daughter joined in.

Such disrespect! I am a graduate with honours! Political Science honours! Very well, I shall start asserting my rights in this house from tomorrow.

After mocking me all they wanted, the duo headed off to bed. Now, with no one around to torment me, I can finally write in peace! Ideas come to me, but somehow I am not able to put them into words. Should I wake up Mapa Ibungo and consult him? Concerning women's rights? No way! I'll never consult a man on such matters. Never!

A couple of yawns came over me. I can't sleep yet! The deadline is near. It's the day after.

Ine Sakhi, the secretary of our locality's women Meira Paibi group and Iche Manitombi, the president, arrive early at our house. I arrange seats for my invitees in order of seniority.

At the appointed hour, without a delay of even a second, a golden ladder shoots down straight from the sky towards our courtyard. One after another, the esteemed guests descend to earth in all their divine glory. Ine Sakhi, Iche Manitombi and I rush out to welcome them. What a serene beauty Lady Sita is! Queen Draupadi, wife of the five Pandavas, also has an alluring charm. Inemton Kunti, with her slender build, carries an exceptionally charming face too. And Lady Rajeshwari, consort of the celebrated flautist of Vrindavan, has a beauty that could mesmerise all of Heaven, Earth and Hell.

The guests take their seats. I see that Inemhal Gandhari's seat is empty, I ask Inemton, 'Didn't my invitation reach Inemhal?'

'Her eyes didn't permit her to travel, dear.'

'Oh ho, yes indeed.'

I grab the microphone and announce, 'Today, I have invited you all, respected Satis, epitomes of piousness and chastity, exemplary models for all women, respected, idolized and worshipped both in heaven and on earth, to seek your valuable opinions on the topic, 'Women's Rights in Hindu Mythology.' I would first like to start with Ichebemma Sita … Ichebemma, what are your thoughts on the practice of Swayamvar where a woman is given away as a prize to a complete stranger?'

She exchanges glances with Ichemma Draupadi seated next to her. I place the microphone right in front of her mouth. Gracefully she cleares her throat and replies calmly, 'In my opinion, it is a beautiful tradition where parents choose the best contender for their daughters and the daughters too honour their wishes.'

'But what if Ravan, Lord of Lanka, had won the contest instead?'

Ichemma is taken aback for a moment.

'Fulfilling a father's wish is the daughter's divine duty,' she reasons.

'Do you agree that the patriarchs of those days didn't give their daughters the right to choose their own partners, and the daughters, in turn, never thought of demanding their right?'

Ichemma Sita doesn't reply but simply nods in silence.

'Thank you so much. I would like to end with just one more question. Those days, Lord Rama repeatedly subjected you to the test of fire to prove your chastity. Do you take that as a threat to your right to life?'

'Since I had never violated my dharma, I never felt threatened.'

Ish, such a terrifying answer! If it had happened in today's times the king would be behind bars and the Sati would have been roasted! Just my opinion.

It is Inemton Kunti's turn next. I set the microphone in front of her.

'Why didn't Inemton claim any sort of privilege from the Sun deity?'

Inemton Kunti's face goes crimson as blood. Everyone stares at me. Ine Sakhi rushes to whisper in my ears, 'Why're you asking such embarrassing questions? Are you trying to give her a heart attack?' I regret it at once.

However, Inemton, being the wise, clever and elegant lady that she is, collects herself and replies, 'He has always been a God to me. I have never considered the Sun deity as my husband.'

'Very well. Thanks a lot, Inemton.'

I have a lot more to ask her. But my first question has made things awkward. Let me move to her daughter-in-law, Panchalini, instead.

'Ichemma, let's assume that you and Karna were madly in love with each other. Would you, then, still agree to become the wife of the five Pandavas after Arjun wins the Swayamvar?'

Ichemma ponders for a while but is poised as she replies, 'My father's wishes are more important than my own desires. And it's my dharma to honour that. My own discontent would just have to be suppressed.'

'When the wicked Dushasana humiliated you publicly in the court, why did you not teach him the lesson that a woman has the right to protect herself?'

'Such things cannot be taught to those who are ignorant of the Dharma Shastra.'

'Very well. Thank you for sharing your views.'

At that moment, Lady Radhika's mobile phone rings inside her bag, *Teet … teet … teet…* Must be a call from Lord Madan Mohan.

'There's nothing to worry about. Lady Durga is with us,' she says into the phone.

'What did he say?' Inemton enquires.

'That it's a land tainted with dark rule, dark laws and dark people who do not respect women. That I shouldn't stay on too long,' Lady Radhika replies.

I realise we are running out of time. I now turn to Ima Saraswati, who with a *veena* in one hand, continuously imparts knowledge to the world. 'Ima Ibemma, do you have any plans to write a book on women's rights in the context of our times?'

Ima Ibemma smiles gracefully and answers, 'I've just finished writing a book titled, *The Rights of Women in the 21st Century*. Right now it is with the Sri Vishwakarma printing press.'

'I would like to thank you for your support towards women's rights', I tell her.

Ima Ibemma Radhika is next. She is the mistress of the cosmos. I must not ask her inappropriate questions.

'Ima Ibemma, we all want our love to belong solely to us. But men go on to break up our preciously-guarded love into pieces and scatter them around. What do you have to say to that?'

'To be honest dear, it's tragic. I have gone through many heartbreaks because of him. One day, I caught him red-handed at Chandrabali's grove. Vishnu! Vishnu! The crown of peacock feathers usually worn on his forehead had ended up at the back of his head. And his golden-coloured silk loincloth had gone up from his waist and wrapped itself around his neck! How I cried! There isn't anyone in the universe who doesn't arouse his fancy. Finally, I learned he is only spreading the joy of love across the universe, granting everyone's wishes.'

'Thank you Ima Ibemma, extremely thankful to you.'

My thoughts wander a bit. '*Ish*! If such generosity was exerted today, quite a lot of girls would have their heads shaved and given away in shotgun marriages', I think to myself.

Expecting to get some bold replies, I hand over the microphone to Ima Durga.

'Ima Ibemma, are you okay with the Divine Father, Lord Shiv Shambhu, spending his entire day stoned? Have you ever felt that you have the right as his consort to voice your likes and dislikes, and thereby try to stop him?'

'Are you kidding me? Those days we didn't have any likes or dislikes. We had never heard of these so called rights and privileges. Forget about asking him to quit. What with that temper of his, on those days when his mood gets extra foul my hands hurt just filling up his chillum.'

Everyone seemed to be amused. I proceed with my next question. 'Do you agree that from time immemorial women have never demanded or got their rights?'

'Nothing's more true than that statement, my dear. That is exactly why I have ten hands and weapons in each of them.'

'We are so pleased with Ima's courageous reply. And now, please give us a piece of advice for the women of today', I requested.

'This is not the time to smile and wilt away like delicate flowers anymore. We must fight for our dignity and rights with the new weapons at hand!' Ima declares.

After interviewing the Satis from Heaven, a new thought strikes me. Why not include an opinion from an earthly Sati? Night after night, Ine Sakhi, the Meira Paibi leader, protects her children, her husband and the honour of women. She patrols the dark streets, torch in hand, and fights the demons who roam about. Surely she is no less a Sati. I take the assembly's permission. All agree, 'Why not? Why not?' I ask her, 'What do you think, Ine?'

'Imaipemma! What do I say?' she exclaims. Taking off the *phi* from her shoulders, she ties it around her waist and stands up purposefully. Microphone in hand, she clears her throat once and fires away, 'Ahem! We have also listened to a lot of scriptures narrated to us. In ancient times, women never got their rights. Dharmaraj Yudhishtira, to whom even the Gods bow their heads in respect, gave away Ibemma Draupadi in a game of dice. Is that ethical? No seriously, are women objects?'

Ichemma Draupadi glares briefly at Ine Sakhi and lowers her head. Ine's speech continues. 'To uphold the dharma of Sati, women were forcibly thrown into the fire. Eh! Good for them it wasn't Sakhi! Wouldn't I have burnt their hands with my flaming torch!'

Except for Ichemma Sita, everyone else looks at Ine with awe. Then abruptly Ine Sakhi declares, 'That's all', and goes back to her chair.

The interview of all the Satis from Heaven as well as earth is over. I proceed with the closing speech. 'After listening to everyone's opinion today, I would like to conclude that there was no mention of women's rights in the ancient Hindu scriptures or mythology. Are we all agreed on that?'

Ima Durga and Ine Sakhi are the only ones to admit courageously, 'Absolutely!' The others simply look at each other. I wait for their response.

'Ibemnungshi, Ibemnungshi! What have you been doing with that pen in hand and drool all over! Get up or the mosquitoes will carry you off.' Mapa Ibungo wakes me up.

If he had waited just five more minutes, my seminar paper would have been complete.

'Now show me what you've been writing.'

'I haven't even started', I reply.

'As expected! Now just go to bed then.'

'No, I shan't sleep tonight. Keep the candle and matchbox here. And please could you have my seminar paper printed early in the morning tomorrow.'

This short story was first published in Manipuri as 'Sati Interview' in the collection of short stories *Naohong*, written by Sanatombi Ningombam, published in 2006 by Siroi Publications, Thoubal, Manipur.

The Debt Repaid

SUNITA NINGOMBAM

Translated from the Manipuri by
NATASHA ELANGBAM

Not a single day passes without Lalita stopping by, on her way to the market, at Shyamo's shop to eat at least one *zarda*-laden *kwa*. Even today, standing in front of the shop at the point where the small lane meets the main road, she says, 'It would be such a relief if I could stop eating your *kwa*. Here, give me one and wrap two more nicely.'

Shyamo smiles. Sprinkling the tobacco, he replies, 'I feel so empty-handed if I don't prepare at least one *kwa* everyday for you, Iteima.' Though unrelated by blood, he calls her 'Iteima', which means elder sister-in-law and is in deference to her husband.

'Really, Shyamo?'

Putting the *kwa* in her mouth, she says, 'I must owe you quite a lot of money by now, how much is it?'

'Not that much yet. Around three hundred and fifty rupees maybe.'

Lalita's eyes widen. She looks around her and says, 'I'll clear it after this coming *Ningol Chakkouba* festival, even if partially. I'll try to pay off the whole amount around Christmas. This is the lean season, clothes are not selling as well as they should.'

'Never mind, it doesn't matter, it's for you. I'm more than satisfied if Iteima just comes and stands in front of my shop.'

'Oh dear, what things you say, you rogue!'

Lalita laughs out loud. Shyamo also joins in the laughter.

Youthful allure has departed from Lalita but one cannot deny her beauty. Her cheeks are sunken, and the skin above her high cheekbones, though it appears fine when at rest, shows a few thin lines at the corner of her eyes when she laughs. But that only adds to her beauty. There's something quite charming in the way she looks and the way she talks. The only thing wanting is that she's a widow.

It hasn't been long since Lalita started eating *kwa*. It was around four or five years back, when she started selling clothes in the market. Her husband, Biramani, was a government clerk at the Electricity Department. Every day Lalita would get ready in time so that the two of them could go to work together. Following Biramani's example, Lalita started eating *kwa* regularly.

After Biramani passed away, she wasn't able to give up the habit. At first, she didn't let her dues build up too much. She would pay when the amount reached ten or twenty rupees. But now, as her dose of *kwa* increased to not less than two or three a day, and expenses rose as her children grew and her income diminished, her debt mounted. Shyamo, who used to sometimes ask for payment when the dues reached fifty or a hundred rupees, had now stopped asking. Instead, he seemed almost embarrassed whenever Lalita brought up the subject of money. Trying to come up with a few meaningful words, he would stutter and blush. Lalita recognized the signs. She smiled inwardly, 'This Shyamo, what does he think he's doing?'

Human hearts are so prone to sins. Among all the living species, if one were to pick the most sinful one, it would be the human species. The more civilized human society, the more self-seeking it becomes; wanting everything to be to their advantage. For the sake of pleasure, they start losing their humanity. It is this that makes human behaviour vile, and corrupts the beauty of our customs and traditions. From a light-hearted exchange, Shyamo starts using innuendo. He loses all inhibition in expressing his heart's desires. Without quite realizing it, Lalita's heart too starts leaning towards Shyamo. But sometimes when her tumultuous heart settles, she wonders: whatever is happening, can this be right? Even with these thoughts, she fails to discipline her wayward mind. Instead it mocks her further, 'Hah! This is becoming quite enjoyable!' But this she forgets – human emotions are not something you can toy with.

That day, Lalita came under a spell. She dreamt with her eyes wide open. It was mid-noon as she had set out a little late for the market. Inside his shop, on the small wooden make-shift platform that he used to sit or rest, lay Shyamo, flat on his back. Seemingly asleep, his eyes were shut. His body was bare except for the pale red-chequered *lungi* wrapped around his waist and covering his lower half. Drops of sweat glistened on a body scorched by the summer sun. Quite forgetting herself, Lalita's gaze fell on his broad chest. Her heartbeat began to sync with the rhythmic rise and fall of Shyamo's breathing. She started to shiver. A hot wave of desire suddenly rose high, burning up her heart. She found herself unable to call out right away and wake him up. His silent, well-built form seems to cast a strange spell on her, making her drowsy in broad daylight. Her eyes became heavy. She stood there for quite a while, gazing at the sleeping form.

'Eh! Iteima!'

Shyamo's startled call brings Lalita back to her senses. She has no time to avert her unguarded gaze. Putting on the undershirt lying beside him, Shyamo says with a laugh, 'Does one who comes to buy something usually remain silent?'

'You looked as if you were fast asleep, just felt bad waking you up.' Lalita's heart is still racing, and her voice quivers. Shyamo immediately grasps the implication of this. Grabbing the opportunity he says, 'Today I'll have to collect the price for stealthily watching someone sleep.'

Lalita is unable to make light of it, her mind and body both drained. But she retorts, 'Don't be so annoying Ibungo, just give me the *kwa*.'

Shyamo suddenly jumps down from his platform and stands in front of Lalita. There is not a soul around. Thinking he's found the long-awaited moment, Shyamo is keen to unburden his importunate heart.

He says, 'Seriously … instead of going to sell clothes at the market, let's run this shop together.'

'Would that be better?'

'It is better, way better.'

Lalita laughs inanely. Encouraged, Shyamo grasps Lalita's outstretched fingers while giving her the *kwa*, and looks intently at her. His gaze meets Lalita's impetuous one.

Sharply retracting her fingers, she scolds him with a trace of anger, 'Go away! How can you, to your Iteima?'

She turns around and marches off. Behind her, Shyamo laughs happily.

Even after reaching the market, Lalita feels as if she is still drifting in a dream. She asks herself: what in the world is happening? In that unchecked moment, the waves of heady desire almost overwhelm her heart. This is not acceptable. She is a married woman, a widow. But how can she restrain herself? Blood flows through her veins too. How can you say that the hearts of those lonely women, those without husbands, have dried up? What should have flowed freely has been dammed up by society and its rules. Behind this barricade, a widow clutches the memory of her lost husband and lets all that flows from her heart stream down as tears. Only then is she called a woman, allowed to live and go about. Today the tide that strained to overflow this barrier almost managed to submerge Lalita up to her neck. Only at this stage did she come to her senses. All this while she had laughed thinking she was toying with Shyamo, but now she realizes that her heart had been involved in the play. She can feel the agony of that. The more she thinks about it, the more disgusted she feels with herself. She curses herself, murmuring, 'Damn it! How could I?'

She remembers the intoxicating *kwa* preparation clutched in her palm. She clenches her fingers. The sweat-drenched *kwa* lies inside still. Shyamo's sweat-glistened body comes to mind again. She begins to shake with repulsion and disgust, and hurls away the *kwa*. She fumes silently. How dare he! To me!

That night, Lalita is restless. Her thoughts in a turmoil, self-reproach fills her heart. She thinks, how filthy can the human heart be? If one were to search for the filthiest place on earth, it must be the human heart. Heart! Is there anyone without a heart? Then, is there anyone who is not filthy? Again she disagrees with herself and shakes her head. She turns on her side and stares unblinking at the innocent face of her youngest son sleeping beside her. She remembers her late husband. In the murky depths of her heart, the pure image of her husband remains intact. Shedding all the tears she had, she starts repenting. She recalls the first night of their life together. Biramani had said, 'Why do I love you so much?' She had laughed tenderly, slightly embarrassed. That love is still deeply etched today; a guy like Shyamo is not worthy of that kind of love.

She gets up suddenly, unable to control her bristling heart, jumps off from the bed and takes out her youngest son's piggy bank. At this late hour, she breaks it open and counts the coins inside. Bobomacha opens his eyes and looks at his mother tearfully, 'Ima, why're you opening my piggy bank? No, don't take out my money.'

Lalita doesn't pay any attention. Bobomacha grabs the coins from his mother. Lalita brushes aside her son's hand and says, 'Be quiet! Ima will be saving something more precious than this for you. Go back to sleep!'

Whether or not Bobomacha understands his mother's words is debatable, but he hears his mother's promise of something more valuable, and watches silently. Looking at the coins, Lalita considers, do I repay my debt with these coins as they are?

Then again she thinks, so what? Even better. Why should I be embarrassed before such a man?

The next day, Lalita takes out some money from the

amount she keeps aside as her market capital. Tying it together with the coins from her son's piggy bank, she heads out to the market with Bobomacha. At Shyamo's shop, she gives the money to her son and says aloud, so that Shyamo can hear, 'Bobomacha, say that Ima's dues for the *kwa* are being paid. And the extra money is the price for kindly allowing Ima to buy *kwa* on credit all this while.'

Such a lengthy speech is beyond little Bobomacha's ability. But Shyamo hears the tone, he understands its meaning too. Today he gives no *kwa* for Lalita, there is no hand in front to give it to. How would it be possible to fit his heart, inflated with his male ego, in little Bobomacha's hands? He touches the coins lying in front of him. He hears their metallic clink. This is not the voice of the Lalita who had enraptured him. It is the debt for the *kwa*, and the price of the unworthy love, paid with interest.

This short story was first published in Manipuri as 'Sendol Shingba' in the collection of short stories *Khongjee Makhol*, written by Sunita Ningombam, published in 1997 by the Manipur Sahitya Samiti, Thoubal. The book won the Sahitya Akademi Award in 2001.

The Day that Dusked at Dawn

GURUARIBAM GHANAPRIYA

Translated from the Manipuri by
AKOIJAM SUNITA

When the taxi jeeps reached our area, I started using them regularly to go to college. Since this service began right from our gate, commuting became very convenient.

That particular day, I was coming back from college as usual. The jeep had initially been quite packed but towards the end of the journey, only four of us were left on board. Just about a quarter of a kilometre away from my house, a woman disembarked. During that brief stop, another youngish looking woman, probably single if her clothes were anything to judge by, scampered up.

'Who's this I wonder? So close to the end of the taxi route!' the thought struck me. She didn't seem to be a local either. I looked at her and wondered if she was in her right mind. The other two co-passengers also seemed to be thinking the same thing because they too looked at her, bewildered. She seemed exhausted, her breath came in gasps. Anxiety cast a shadow on her face. Her hair was still dripping wet but she had tied it up into a bun at the nape of her neck. Her clothes also seemed damp. But she was pleasing to look at – neither too young nor too mature. Her beauty was not the soft and tender beauty often ascribed to a woman. Instead, something in her spoke of both strength and bravery. Her demeanour that day – the way she sat huddled in a corner without even looking at the road ahead – hinted at a story. I yearned to know the reason, but how was I to ask?

The jeep reached our gate. Everyone got down. The driver started collecting the fares. I glanced back; she was still seated inside.

As I opened the gate to my house, she called out, 'Ibemma'.

I stopped and turned back. Stepping out of the jeep, she said, 'Is this your home?'

'Yes.'

'Come, let's go inside.'

She went through the gate ahead of me. I was baffled – what was going on?

'How many siblings do you have?' she asked as we walked together.

'I'm an only child.'

'What does your father do?'

'He is a Section Officer at the Secretariat.'

'Today Iche will sit at your place for a while.' She had already assumed the title of elder sister, attributing me the role of the younger one: Inao. I didn't respond. An unknown fear slowly crept into my mind. I asked myself again, 'Who is she?'

I headed straight to my room. She followed close behind. I kept my college bag on the table, and then, even though it was my home, I stood there perplexed, not knowing what to do. Sensing my confusion, she said, 'You must be surprised. Here, I'll tell you everything.'

She then narrated her story. Though my initial surprise disappeared after I listened to her, I was still perplexed.

'Do you have a phone at home?'

'Yes.'

'Where is it? I need to make a call.'

'In the next room, Iche. Go in and use it. There's no one else at home.'

She went into the next room just as my mother came back home.

'You're home, Ibemma?'

'Yes, Ima.'

'Then change your clothes and have your food. Why're you standing there transfixed like a tree?'

Ima began scolding non-stop as usual. Then, noticing me place my index finger on my lips, gesturing to her to be silent, she stopped mid-speech and looked at me, bewildered. Suddenly, now, she seemed to hear the phone conversation going on in the next room. She took a quick look inside and then, turning to me, mouthed, 'Who?' tilting her head in the direction of the sound.

'Seems to be a member of a revolutionary group', I whispered back.

'What? How is she here?'

I briefly recounted the story to my mother, 'She'd contracted malaria and had to come out of her camp for treatment. Three or four of them were surrounded while taking refuge in a house nearby. Fortunately, at that time, she was bathing by the pond in one corner of the homestead.

When she heard the commotion, she looked towards the house and saw it was surrounded by the police.'

'Right! Just a while back we heard some gunshots. That must have been it. But how is she here?'

'She escaped, crossing through the neighbouring houses to reach the road. There, she boarded the jeep I was travelling in, and that's how she ended up here.'

At that moment she came out from the room, putting an end to our conversation. She asked my mother, 'Ima, are you Ibemma's mother?'

'Yes, I am.'

'I shan't be staying long. Once the uproar settles down a bit, they'll certainly send someone to pick me up. I'll have to bother you two for some three or four hours. I hope you don't mind.'

'Why would we mind?'

Iche seemed to gauge that though Ima might not have minded, she was petrified and extremely anxious. She said, 'Please don't be afraid, Ima. I'll not do anything to involve anyone from this house.'

The sight of her still dressed in her damp clothes made me feel bad. I gave her a top and a *phanek* to change into.

I was in a fix, unsure of what to do or what to talk about. Her presence made me uneasy and fearful. But she did not seem to be affected by anything although she did look out of the window every now and again.

I desperately searched for a means to go out.

'Iche, please make yourself comfortable', I said and tried to get out from the room.

'Are you busy?'

'No, not at all.'

'Then sit here with me for a while.'

Either it was her nature or she was trained well, but for a moment I was bewitched by her words. All my discomfort and unease quickly faded. As the relaxed mood grew, I asked, 'Iche, where is your home?'

She didn't answer immediately, just looked at me intently.

'Do you want to know who I am?'

I didn't respond.

She continued, 'I am a soldier fighting for freedom.'

'Iche, do you think you'll win?'

'Defeats are for those who run away from the battlefield. The one who rejects subjugation and embraces death is a victorious soldier.'

As she spoke, her eyes became bloodshot and her breathing quickened. She struggled to remain calm and continued, 'Therefore, I…'

Before she could finish, there was the sound of a horn outside. She stood up at once, and looked out through the window. She said, 'They've come for me. I'll go now. I've put you to enough trouble. May God bless you!'

The next morning, as I came out to pray to the Sun, the day's newspaper was lying on the verandah. I couldn't bring myself to walk past it. Quickly I scanned through the front page. The headline read: 'Woman leader of a revolutionary group, Pecha Liklai Chanu killed in encounter with the Central Reserve Police Force.' A large photo accompanied the news. Goosebumps rose all over my body at the sight.

'Alas! So early in the day. So beautiful and strong, and so brave … what a loss.'

This short story was first published in Manipuri as 'Nongallakpada Mamshinkhraba Nongma' in the collection of short stories *Thamoigi Leeching*, written by Guruaribam Ghanapriya, published in 2001 by Kumari Maibam Chandani Devi for Progressive Publication Society, Manipur.

Nightmare

NEE DEVI

Translated from the Manipuri by
SOIBAM HARIPRIYA

Somo sinks down into the sofa as soon as they enter. She looks at Leishna who follows close behind, notices her downcast face and asks suspiciously, 'What took you so long?'

Leishna doesn't reply, unable to decide what exactly to say. She sits down beside Somo, her ears still smarting.

'Why're you here? Why don't you come after I die?'

Leishna's mother had lost all hope of seeing her daughter. Yet the moment she saw her after such a long time she shouted at her, raising her feeble voice as much as she could.

Leishna doesn't confront her mother. Holding herself back, she sits down, her face lowered, on the bed laid opposite to where her mother lies.

After a few moments of quietude, her mother starts again without even looking at her, 'We were waiting for you to come to your senses on your own, but you, as time goes by, you've forgotten yourself more and more! You think it's possible to live life the way you imagine it in your mind?'

Leishna, who's been keeping her emotions in check, lifts her face and retorts, 'Is this why you called me here?'

'Yes, only for that', breathing heavily, Leishna's mother glares at her daughter.

'I am not a child anymore, Ima', Leishna replies in a low but firm voice. 'I can take care of myself.'

'Don't you speak like that, you freak! You must be an eyesore to *that person*'s parents, and how exasperated they must be. They must be berating us, saying what kind of parents gave birth to someone like you. It's because of that I'm saying this. If you can get people to say we are not your parents, you can do as you wish.'

Holding herself back, as her mother pauses for breath, Leishna counters weakly, 'To claim no kinship with you, let me just die then.'

'Die!' Veins throbbing, her mother rasps out loud, 'Instead of living and dragging your parents down, just die! For the inconceivable, why raise such a huge ruckus! Others watch you two like you're some entertainment show. Are you even aware of that?'

Her face burning, Leishna finds it hard to remain seated.

But her mother isn't finished yet. 'People getting married, settling down, having children, do you think it's because of lust? So that children become your refuge when you are old, that is why people have children. Everyone was young once, we've all experienced desire and love. Shameless! Who walks around with their clothes hanging on their arms like you two instead of wearing them? Do you think that is even human behaviour?'

Leishna stands up abruptly to pace up and down the small room. Then, taking out some money from her bag, she approaches her mother. She tries to say something but no words come out of her mouth.

Meanwhile, her mother is not done venting all that has been brewing inside her for so long. Glancing briefly at her daughter from the corner of her eyes, she continues, 'Do you even know how difficult a woman's life is? If married to a good man, even the worst of women get some respect. People think about how her husband will react if they say or do anything against her, and they remain quiet. But if it is an inadequate husband, people don't respect even the woman married to him. What about you? What can your make-believe husband do?'

'Stop it, Ima, stop', Leishna almost shouts with a burst of determination, 'Don't be so ungrateful. That person provided for me, made me what I am. I can never forget that. What man will do likewise for me? If I had remained in this house, would I ever have reached where I am today? And if I had not got so far, what man would have desired me today? Ima, just think about it.' She throws the money onto the bed and turns her head away.

Leishna's mother had been watching her, her brows knotted with fury. She exclaims bitterly, 'So, if anyone asks the name of your man, should I say – *Somorani*?'

Leishna covers hear ears with her hands, her eyes brimming with tears. As she walks towards the door, her frail mother suddenly stands up. She scoops up the money and flings it towards her daughter.

'What're you thinking?'

Leishna wakes up from her reverie at the question. Glancing

once at Somo, she lets out a heavy sigh. Then coiling up her hair into a bun, she slowly walks towards the kitchen.

They had gone to Leishna's house to ask after her ailing mother. Somo didn't go in, staying behind in the car parked at the gate. As soon as Leishna came out, they had driven off without a word. Nor did they converse during the ride back.

Somo stretches out on the sofa. Leishna brings in two steaming cups of tea. Sitting down, she announces, 'They asked me to stay over today.'

Somo sits up, surprised. She asks, 'Who said that?'

'Ibungo', Leishna replies, looking away. 'No one else spoke a word to me.'

'And your mother?'

'She was angry. She threw away the money I gave her, and told me to come after her death', she narrates bits and parts of the story. 'Her heath had deteriorated a lot.'

After a brief silence, Somo asks faintly, 'What did you tell them?'

Leishna breathes deeply. Softly she answers, 'I am thinking of going there tomorrow…'

Somo doesn't reply for a while. Then she suggests, 'How about you go in the morning and return here at night?' She waits for a response, looking at Leishna.

Turning her face away, Leishna replies, 'They said she wakes up frequently during the night.'

'All those people in the house are not enough?' Somo sits up now.

'Since her illness has lasted quite a while, it seems they're all worn-out.' Passing the tea, Leishna continues, 'Even for going to the bathroom and such things, they tell me someone is always required to be around her.'

Somo takes the tea and stares vacantly for a while. Then she says, 'That's fine by me…'

Leishna went home for a few days. She took only a few clothes with her.

Somo counted the days of her absence. What was most unbearable for her was the slow darkening of the day into dusk, that time when everyone returned to their homes. Every evening, she would stand for hours at the door to their room on the upper floor of the family house – watching the silent hills afar, the birds flying homewards after the days' quest for food, the clouds disappearing before her eyes into the darkness. Waking up in the morning and finding Leishna still in deep slumber, rousing her and lecturing her on the ills of waking up late, and before sleep – about eating, dressing, friends, films, sports, songs and entertainment, or else the events of the world – picking up any of these topics and discussing them with her in detail – these were all habits ingrained in Somo.

Since the time they started living together, the clothes she wore, the food she ate, the work she took up – Leishna played a great role in all of this. Every item in the room, in all nooks and corners, Leishna's influence was evident. The time without her made everything seem incomplete and meaninglessness to Somo. These last few days didn't even seem real; she'd never thought such a day would come. In such an empty and lonely world, how could Somo possibly live!

During Leishna's absence she felt acutely the stares of her own family members who disapproved of their union, and had become strangers to her. Mixed with her anguish was the unbearable shame of having been let down. She wanted to conceal herself from all prying eyes. Hiding from the eyes of

Somo's father and siblings, her mother would furtively come to the door or windows, and peek in to inquire – have you eaten? Today Somo felt embarrassed at this concern coming from the mother whom she had forgotten when she was together with Leishna. It touched her heart deeply. But she didn't want to reveal her weakness either. All these have to be suppressed. At this behaviour, her mother would also leave silently most times.

'All this is so very entertaining, your spectacle!'

Lying down on the bed fully clothed as soon as she returned from work, Somo seemed to have drifted off to sleep. She saw her mother put down the plate of food she'd brought with her, and felt a pang in her heart. She immediately closed her eyes again. Reaching for a towel nearby, she placed it over her already closed eyes.

'If she's not here, do you have to forgo eating? Will you fast to death too?' Somo's mother mutters, tidying the clothes that lie about haphazardly. 'We've grown tired waiting so long for this eclipse to end just so that we could do a purifying ritual.'

Somo who's been lying on her back, turns on her side to face the wall. Now, there are no words to say it. No courage either. Nor the desire to speak.

Her mother continues, 'Forcing yourself into someone's house, behaving in the manner of a home-breaker daughter-in-law, she came in between parent and offspring, separated siblings… Aren't people diffident and bashful when young? At her age, when asked my name, I couldn't even respond and give my name… That woman, if tomorrow she doesn't break up her husband's home after she marries, I swear to God I'll kill myself.'

A kind of disquiet settles in Somo's heart. She suddenly remembers her mother's words, 'When she gets married and you are left high and dry, that's when I'll clap my hands and laugh…'

She hasn't given any attention to these words earlier. But now, she feels goosebumps rising. Suddenly she wants her mother to go away. She lets out a deep breath and says, almost pleading, 'Leave me alone, Ima.'

Her mother turns away swiftly, and walks out, saying, 'The bags of money that we spent in nurturing you, was it for you to rear this witch? Since you're being spirited away by this enchantress, right now your eyes and ears are closed. You'll continue living in your dreamland. One day when she, satiated after taking all that she can from you, takes flight, that's when you'll realise. That time you'll know. Mark my words. It isn't long before my prediction will be proved right!'

Somo had never allowed anyone to even cast a harsh glance at Leishna. For her sake, out of her own jealousy, she herself had been caught in many embarrassing situations. But today as her mother criticised Leishna to her heart's content, she listened to it all helplessly. And, after cutting off all ties with her own family and offering everything to Leishna without keeping back even a fragment for herself, Somo now silently bore the pain of having been abandoned. The words that often rose in her heart unexpectedly, regardless of time or place, sound again on her lips – 'Leishna, do you mean to kill me?'

Somo can't stem her tears. She wants to cry out loud. She wants to set out that very instant and bring Leishna back, snatching her from the hands of her parents. Her heart fills with condemnation – this society, how many obstacles it creates in the private lives of others, how much it wants to hold other's rights in its fist, what kind of society is this! This tradition which decides that unless the union is of a man and a woman, two people can't become life partners – what kind of oppressive tradition is this? Are the bonds of the body priced higher than those of the heart? Love is a manifestation of the inner soul; has it become an expression merely of the outward appearance? Does love have to depend on the approval or disapproval of others?

For Somo, life itself has been a test of life and death. At the same time, it is also a strong challenge. Her challenge comes not only from her kith and kin, or from society but also from herself, her mannerisms, her conduct and her own body. Somo, who doesn't recall wearing a *phanek* since birth, might not have thought of herself as a man; but she had never considered herself a woman either. With her innate strength and courage, she had always triumphed over the neighbourhood boys of her age. She grew up in the company of boys. Her grandfather used to say, 'My grandchild is not a female, she is a male.' Thus encouraged, she had always harboured masculine thoughts, and had always been taught the duties and trades of a man. Had her grandfather's exhortations spurred on what was already there in her blood?

Leishna came after about a week. As soon as she reached, she started cleaning the room – sweeping, mopping and dusting in all corners without a moment's rest. She did the laundry and asked if Somo had been eating regularly. She did not, however, mention if her mother had recovered from her illness or not.

That night how serenely and contentedly Leishna had slept besides her. And how lovingly Somo had gazed at her! Looking at her tender face as she slept like a child, Somo recalled the time when Leishna's sister had called her on the pretext of sharing a meal together and tried to forcibly marry her off to someone. It was as if the whole incident had happened only yesterday.

That day, though Somo hadn't been able to gather strength and do something for her sake, she had held the quivering Leishna's hands and in an equally quivering voice said, 'You, you alone do not change. You alone stand steady. The day you turn away, that will be my last day. That is the only thing I fear.'

The vow Leishna made that day, and how she had escaped from the clutches of her own family for her – this had filled Somo's heart with pride as if it was her own victory, as if a test has been irrevocably overcome. They had held each other tight, as if no power in this world could tear them apart again.

Somo continued to gaze at Leishna, slowly caressing her hair.

The next day, Leishna's younger brother came to fetch her. When she noticed that Leishna betrayed neither fear nor reluctance at leaving her side, a terrible pain stabbed through Somo's heart. She wanted to say so much but she did not utter a word. She noticed that Leishna took along a few more clothes than normal and was suspicious. But again, she thought it might be her own weakness.

A few days later Leishna came for a day again, accompanied by her sister. Immediately Somo remembered how every time Leishna went to her home she had escorted her, how she had never left her unaccompanied.... All of Somo's eagerness vanished on seeing these changes. The whole world appeared to her like a pretence, filled with betrayal and deception.

Leishna sits with her head hung low, across the table from Bikash. After a while, she lifts her head and is about to take the cup of coffee in her hands when she sees Somo striding purposefully towards her, seething with anger, her eyes bloodshot and glaring. Leishna instantly jerks upright from her seat, her heart pounding against her chest. Somo reaches the table and stands firmly in front of her, visibly trying to control her fury. Leishna remains standing on unsteady legs, unable to meet her eyes. Somo raises a trembling hand to Leishna's chin and slowly tilts up her bowed face. Her glowering eyes bore into Leishna's eyes.

Bikash, who has been watching the unfolding events astounded, stands up immediately.

Somo's intense eyes begin to fill up with tears. She suddenly raises a quivering, unsteady hand and slaps Leishna across her face. And then without a word, without lingering for even a second more, she turns and leaves.

Bikash, stunned for a while, takes a step towards the departing Somo.

'No, No, this is not her fault. It's me. I'm the one who's wrong,' With anguished sobs, Leishna restrains Bikash. Hiding her face in her hands, she starts weeping bitterly.

For the second or the third time today, Somo's mother stands near the door trying to wake her up. After going out briefly in the afternoon, she had come back and locked herself in. At night, though her mother had called out many times to give her food, Somo had refused to open the door. Faint strains of music could be heard till the late hours of the night.

Somo's mother climbs up the stairs yet again, scolding under her breath. She stands near the door and calls out, 'Somo, Somorani ... it's almost noon, are you dead?'

No response from the room. Somo's mother has never encountered her offspring waking up so late, and she feels a stab of worry in her heart. She steps closer and nudges the door a bit. The door which has been tightly shut since the previous day suddenly opens on its own. A pungent smell immediately envelops her. Anxiety creeps up in her heart. Covering her nose with a corner of her wrap, she slowly enters the room and looks around.

Somo lies face down and unmoving across the middle of the vast bed, seemingly asleep. She doesn't seem to have bothered to pull down the mosquito net the previous night. Seeing an empty glass bottle and a tumbler in front of the bed, Somo's mother bends down and looks closely at the bottle. Photo albums, their pages open, and some loose photographs lie scattered all around the bed. Still looking at the photos her mother calls out again, 'Somo, Somorani... Do you hear me?'

Somo does not respond.

Her mother suddenly notices a few empty tablet strips among the scattered photographs. Picking them up, she looks intently at them, and then turns towards her child again. Shaking her body, she tries to wake her up, 'Somo, Somo...!'

Somo does not budge even a bit.

Agitated, Somo's mother strokes her cheeks. They are as cold as ice. Slowly she caresses her child's face again. Something lies buried under her face. Lifting her head a bit, she removes it. It is a framed photograph of Leishna. Wildly flinging it away, she embraces her child tight. She turns her eyes upwards for a second, transfixed and unblinking. Then she starts wailing her heart out, 'Somo … Somorani.'

This short story was first published in Manipuri as 'Manglaknaba' in the collection of short stories *Lei Mana Amatang*, written by Nee Devi, published in 2009 by Ng. Gung-gung on behalf of Writers' Forum, Manipur.

The Defeat

NINGOMBAM SURMA

Translated from the Manipuri by
BOBO KHURAIJAM

The function will begin at one o'clock. And it's already noon.
But Bipin is still not home. When he set off for work this
morning, Nalini had said, 'Please make sure you're back before
noon. There are many important people coming today.'

So, why isn't he back? Nalini searches hard for a possible
explanation for his non-arrival, but that only serves to
increase her despair. Who would believe that a littérateur like
Bipin would take today's event so lightly? Today, Nalini, his
wife, who recently received a prestigious award, is going to
be felicitated. His wife. She will go up on stage and say a
few words, and then she'll tell everyone how the sole credit
for her achievement goes to her husband ... surely Bipin
will be interested in hearing these words? Thus far, he's
done everything that is possible for her. He chides her often,
'Why so careless with spellings? Be very careful, also with

expressions. A beautiful storyline, some beautiful words by themselves are not enough. Also, be attentive to the economy of words.'

Bipin is never careless about anything. Whenever Nalini completes a piece, he reads it at least once and then makes a few changes – he's been doing this religiously, as if it is what he must do, a duty.

He says, 'Without the help and support of men, all of women's powers and skills will be wasted. Because, at present, women lag far behind in social status.'

His analytical book on feminism has received a lot of praise. Besides, his anthology of poems which dealt with women's issues has been acknowledged as a very outstanding book – even regarded as being capable of empowering women to draw forth their hidden strength. Some literary organisations in Manipur have honoured him with awards for his work. That has reinforced his standing as a leading feminist. Bipin also helps Nalini with the household chores, and supports her in many other ways. He believes that confining her to the innumerable yet miniscule household chores can lead to domestic discord, and perhaps even a distance between them.

He often says, 'Without the sincerity of a true feminist, it is not possible to do justice to a discussion on feminism. Only those who truly believe in uplifting women, and are able to look at them with love, are able to discuss feminism in literature.'

When they hear him talk like this, some women are not without envy. 'Had we received support from our men like her, we too would have scaled great heights.'

That is their opinion. Nalini too is in agreement. Why should she not be proud? How many women like her have husbands who say, 'It is necessary that we have our women wield the pen instead of the ladle and tongs, and make them come out.'

When Bipin received an award, Nalini's fellow women writers had remarked, 'Our society badly needs more men like him. This is an occasion for us to celebrate his well-written book on women's issues.'

How she had swelled with pride at that. She was so happy. After all, a wife's pride at her husband's achievements was only natural!

Nalini is being felicitated today for the prestigious national-level literary award she recently received for her third book. With that achievement she has suddenly become a respected and important literary figure, having carved a niche for herself. Following the award her days have been filled with receptions in her honour.

Bipin too has become quite immersed in work. He leaves home at sunrise and comes back after sunset. As a result, they haven't been able to attend many events together. When she asks him, his standard reply is, 'It's the end of the financial year in the office.'

Yesterday, she had pleaded, 'Please don't go to work tomorrow, everyone will ask about you.'

'There's an important party to celebrate our boss's promotion.'

'No! I insist we go together tomorrow.'

'Look, if I don't go, Biren will be upset. Today too, it was just the two of us taking care of the preparations for tomorrow's party. Besides, the boss will also question my absence.'

'Tell him the reason', Nalini retorted.

Bipin only smiled in reply and went out. He did not have

the courage to refuse Nalini's entreaties. And his little smile gave Nalini a ray of hope. So, this morning, she had dared to insist again, 'Please make sure you're back before noon. There are many important people coming today.' Bipin hadn't said he wouldn't.

Nalini believed that Bipin would be back in time. Why wouldn't he? He had helped her immensely to reach this stage. Though he had missed her felicitation events earlier, surely he wouldn't want to miss today's?

Has he forgotten? Quite unlikely. Something must have cropped up. She kept wondering what. A fair bit of time elapsed in this mental turmoil. It was getting quite late by then. Nalini got dressed. After a little while, she made her decision and headed out.

Nalini trusts Bipin. This person who has stood by her side at various points in their lives, she didn't want to put him to the test of trust. These are words that Bipin often uses, 'To forgo a trust kept cherished for a lifetime because of a fleeting incident would be stupidity. There will always be a reason behind every incident.'

At the felicitation, everything happens in a daze. Bipin doesn't turn up till the end. Worry mixes with self-pity in her head. Nalini can't recollect her own speech during the event. She reaches home on the verge of tears, but Bipin still hasn't come back.

It is well over nine o'clock when Bipin returns that night. Nalini feels that today she might not be able to control herself and will surely burst into tears.

'Have you eaten?'

No answer. He continues, 'Didn't I tell you not to wait for me? I told you to have your dinner.'

The explanation rises silently in Nalini's mind, 'These things, like me waiting for you or wanting to have dinner with you, you won't be able to change saying you are a feminist. These things really depend on how you feel.'

Aloud, her voice laden with unshed tears and anger, she says, 'Your party which began early in the morning ended just now?'

Women are well-versed in such questions that are aimed at starting an argument. They also know the answer very well. But Nalini heard a different answer today, 'I'm very tired. This … I can't bear this.'

Nalini looks at Bipin, astonished. What is it that he is unable to bear? What had happened? Bipin had once said, 'I love people; I wouldn't like to do anything that would hurt anybody or bring grief to anyone.' It is because of such words that Nalini has the highest of regard for him. What is more valuable than a heart that holds love for everyone?

'What happened?'

'Nothing. Why?'

But writ large on Bipin's face is the shadow of an anxiety, a certain restlessness. Nalini can't accept that nothing has happened. It is not just today or yesterday that they've known each other; they've been together for many years. However, true to her nature, she doesn't probe further. Her silence unsettles Bipin even more.

'Silence is also a kind of conceit. I want to live with dignity. I am a man.'

This time a stab of pain shoots through Nalini's heart. Bipin seems to be saying, 'You taking me wherever you wish, making me stand anywhere you wish, all these I won't agree to. I am a man; I do not wish to stand behind you and be introduced by you to those who are felicitating you.'

In her writings Nalini had dwelt at length on different facets of the human heart. But she has failed to understand the heart of someone so close to her. Nalini begins to realise – the award that she had received was not due to her achievement, but because of her defeat.

This short story was first published in Manipuri as 'Maithiba' in the collection of short stories *Ethak Machasinggi Wahang*, written by Ningombam Surma, published in 2007 by the author herself for Khorjeiroi Khutmarup, Manipur.

Monthly Flower

HAOBIJAM CHANU PREMA

Translated from the Manipuri by
THINGNAM ANJULIKA SAMOM

That day I still recall,
A Diwali afternoon
While I listened to the Sunday radio drama
You
Appeared for the first time in my life.

In the riverbed with my girlfriends
Happiness overflowing
Swimming, dipping, playing,
When suddenly wanting to go for the big one,
Head to toe, my whole body
Fully drenched, I ran up
And in our latrine
Walled with hedge-plants
While I squatted, listening to the radio drama

You had
Made my heart jump.

Oh, Monthly Flower!
Seeing you
The hair on my scalp rose
Ho, Mother! Is it a leech bite?
Soaked in sweat
How I shook in fright,
I recall as if 'twas yesterday.

Frightened to tell my mother
Befuddled, bewildered
Even the Diwali lights
Couldn't brighten up
Those dark thoughts besieging me.
Tossing to the south
Turning to the north
Sitting up suddenly again
Burying my face in the pillow
Tucking in my *phanek* once more
That night which refused to dawn
How hard I endured that night!

It was Gobardhon Puja day.
To worship the cow
To decorate the house, or the rice-storing pot
I didn't go as usual
To every marigold plant.
Going straight to my Indomcha
I sat there by her side fearfully.

Should I reveal or not
Weighed down by that huge mountain of thoughts.
She, my mother's sister, stringing her garlands
Didn't notice my despairing face.
After sitting for a long time
Looking for a private moment
Apprising her of the matter
I asked her what could be the reason?
'Crazy girl!
If it was a leech
Would you be sitting thusly?
It must be *that* matter
I'll tell my sister for you!'

How restless I was
How depressed I was!

Ima's ears having been notified
She roared,
'Ibemma, come quick!'
My heart racing
Like one at fault
Stood I before my mother.
How vilely she looked at me,
Her daughter now budding
Like once she had bloomed.
Thinking of me as one blossoming in a planting-hole
How cruelly she treated me,
Maybe fear-filled herself
That with the household chores
There won't be any helper,

174

When I too, like her, start blooming
I will go to the beloved's side.

Oh Monthly Flower,
These long years
You remain a burden.
From one moon to another
Difficult if you come, problematic if you don't.
Father, brothers cook in the kitchen
I prepare the vegetables
Barred from the kitchen for all to see
Unable to eat or drink properly
Those times spent
Recalls them today too, this reminiscing mind.

Each time you bloom
My soft inner body
As if pierced by thorns,
As if sliced by sharp knives,
With so much pain I endured!
Studying for the exams,
Couldn't concentrate.
Teachers' lectures,
Couldn't understand.
Unable to sleep,
Unable to go about.

One day too
When none in the world was home
For your sake, I had endured
Almost the last breath.

'Inamma, Inamma, Ima, Ima'
Though long I cried out
For my sister-in-law, my mother,
That day, none was there to hear.
Such harsh pain
Never had I encountered in this lifetime.
A she-devil's nails
As if tore up all arteries and nerves
Groaning in pain
Tears streaming from my eyes
How I had bore it all, groaning and shouting
'Twas for your sake only.

If, at that very moment Ima hadn't returned,
If I hadn't taken a sip of the Panthou Meitei Maiba's
Decoction of the *kwa-manbi* seeds,
It would have been my last moment
Together my mother and the fatherly medicine-man
Gave birth to me anew.

Oh, Monthly Flower!
One day,
My mother
Received you harshly.
In contrast to her fear
I, her daughter,
After knowing you
Even though many seasons went by
Towards the house
Of her son-in-law, I didn't head.
She, losing the fire

176

Of her anger
In its stead
Started shooing me away
To go to my beloved's side
Fearing my spinsterhood.

Monthly Flower,
But you, even today,
Haven't put me at ease.
'Studious one, wealthy one' – happy at the epithets
My mother's shouts have diminished in volume.
Yet you still
Unappeased,
Make me roll about frequently
In pain.

Not only in this present life
But also for the life to come
Filling me with anxiety.
For what reason, you'd,
As though no other days were there,
On a New Moon day, on a Sunday
Appeared for the first time?
That lunar phase, that day
Being one I'm unable to forget
How troubled it made me!
At every glance of the astrologer's book
Always was written clearly
'If a girl's first monthly flower
Appears on a New Moon, or a Sunday
She becomes a widow; her husband's lifespan shortens.'

Oh, Monthly Flower!
Even if I decide against believing,
Since I have grown up amidst this belief,
These words haunt repeatedly
My brooding mind.
For your sake,
Because of you,
The one who's my heart,
How can I send to Death's kingdom?
How will I remain,
All alone in this world
Like a solitary bird flying?

Oh torturous Monthly Flower,
How wicked you are!
Why did you make,
Not only my body-cage
But also my mind restless?

This poem was first published in Manipuri as 'Tha-gi Lei' in the anthology *Punshi Khongchatsida* in 2011 by The Cultural Forum Publications, Manipur.

I Will No Longer Join the Women's War

HAOBIJAM CHANU PREMA

Translated from the Manipuri by
THINGNAM ANJULIKA SAMOM

Don't invite me again, my dear friend
'Let's go join the Nupi Lan'
I'll send my man
Being the strong one, that he is
Having fought in many battles
Way back, from the Stone Age!
Why would I make him ashamed
Nay, I can't do that!

A used knife is sharp.

My Meitei Lion, The Brave!
To make him a knife lying under the bed, useless
To make him the object of ridicule by others

Nay, Ita, I can't
I can't ever do that.

This poem was first published in Manipuri as 'Eidi Nupi Lan Yaoraroi' in the anthology *Sheireng Sheireng* in 2013 by *The Mapao*, a biannual literary journal, Manipur.

A Market Story

KUNDO YUMNAM

'A market story' is about a married Meitei woman who goes to the market (*keithel*) to buy weekly groceries but is instead confronted with a lot of annoying queries which stem from the fact that she dresses and behaves differently from a traditional Meitei *Mou* (married woman). Her clothes, her lack of bangles, the fact that the child is looked after by the father, the fact that she eats beef, and so on. make the two market women throw questions at her which expose their prejudices. She retorts half-heartedly, walks away, and moves on. She is used to it.

Y THE WAY, WHO'S GOING O EAT ALL THOSE VEGETABLES? OW MANY MEMBERS ARE THERE IN THE FAMILY?
IT'S JUST THE FIVE OF US. CAN'T COME OUT OF THE HOUSE OFTEN SO I HAVE TO BUY A WEEK'S VEGETABLES.
HO ALL ARE THERE? ATHER-IN-LAW?
HE HAD PASSED AWAY A LONG TIME AGO.
THERE'S ME, MY HUSBAND, THE TODDLER, BROTHER-IN-LAW......
HOW MUCH FOR THESE?
CAN YOU WAIT FOR A WHILE?
YOU SHARE THE KITCHEN WITH YOUR BROTHER-IN-LAW?
YES
WHAT ABOUT YOUR MOTHER-IN-LAW?

The Skin of a Woman

NATALIDITA NINGTHOUKHONGJAM

If you think about it, scientifically,
it should be unproblematic enough.

But you don't; that makes it tough.

The skin of a woman should, first of all,
be smooth, not rough. Properly moisturised:
knees, elbows, and ankles. Emphatically.
It must be spotless,
carefully coloured in the right places,
full of warmth in tight spaces.

The skin of a woman must resemble hills:
undulating, patient under the sheets. Sentient
to a titillating touch. Lenient as the stem of a bud.
It should be held up by satin and lace
for certain eyes only.

Yet skin is skin, and the skin of a woman
      bears the scars of a knife,
      criss-crossing the top of the fingers.
      It carries the smell of potatoes and fish.
      It reeks of sweat, musky and thick,
      stains the satin and lace, falling from grace.

Skin is skin, and the skin of a woman is not skin
      if hairy or bulging
      where it shouldn't be
      if hairless or hollow
      where it shouldn't be.

The skin of a woman is hated for being skin
      when hidden from an eager view
      when exposed to an eager view.

The skin of a woman is spat upon
      if shared without sanctity.
The skin of a woman is torn apart
      if sharing is restricted.

The skin of a woman is a giver of life,
a shield from bullets,
virginal bait,
cultural gate,
      a selective wet dream
      and collective nightmare.

This poem was originally written in English in 2018. It has not been
published elsewhere before.

Breaking the Shame

YUIMI VASHUM

When I cut my fingers or skin my knees
My mother (s) tell me, '*Put betadine over your wounds*'
And fusses over my sloppiness
Discussing it at the dinner table like I lost a limb.

Yet they refuse to talk about my *vagina*;
Of the *men that abused me* ad infinitum,
Trying to shove their *penis* into my mouth
In the death of the night,
Creeping up to me like the monster under my bed!

Did they know? Did they know?
Was it shame? Was it disgust?
I buried myself in a field of *cosmos*
Playing with it as I plucked off the petals,
Chanting …
Did they know? Did they not know?

Hidden behind a piece of cloth,
They talked about it in hushed tones.
Why would mother (s) not talk about the *vagina*?
Don't they know it's as important as my *limbs*?
Why will they not tell me
To scream and sprint if someone tries to put their hands in my
underwear?
Why?

But not anymore,
Not on my watch.

I will teach my daughter to own every part of her body.
From the roots of her hair to the tip of her toenails.
My daughter will be strong, not meek;
Earn respect not take; give only when deserved.

My daughter shall fight against silence;
So shall my daughter's daughter…
Until there is no shame in the *truth*.

This poem was originally published in English as 'Breaking the Shame' in the collection of poems *Love. Lust. And Loyalty*, written by Yuimi Vashum, published in 2018 by PenThrill Publication Houses, Nagaland.

Here I am, After All These Years

YUIMI VASHUM

You are staring at me
Gleaming with an unspoken question –
Why speak up now, after all these years?
You don't have to raise your hand to have that answered,
I'll tell you, seated.

For centuries
Our mothers spent years mute – saving words to resist;
Stomached assault – saving the courage to rise;
Walked on thorns with bloodied feet – saving the
endurance to win;
Saving it all, for sons and daughters.

Today I break the chain,
I spend the words our mothers had saved –
I gather the century long courage –
I round up endurance.

Today, I spend it all
Lest my children grow *Mute*
Spineless
Submissive.
I spend it all
And refuse to be our mothers
Who accept injustice like a birthright.

Today, I speak
And *reclaim* the voice our mothers long buried.

This poem was originally published in English as 'Here I am, after all these years' in the collection of poems *Love. Lust. And Loyalty*, written by Yuimi Vashum, published in 2018 by PenThrill Publication Houses, Nagaland.

Notes on Authors

Dr Arambam Ongbi Memchoubi (1955 -), who also writes as Thounaojam Chanu Ibemhal, is a poet, critic and researcher based in Imphal. A retired teacher and prolific writer, she has eight poetry collections to her credit – *Nonggoubi* (1984), *Androgi Mei* (1990), *Sandrembi Cheishra* (1993), *Eigi Palem Nungshibi* (1998), *Idu Ningthou* (2005), *Leisang* (2008) and *Tuphai O! Ningthibi* (2012). Her other works include the short story collection *Leiteng* (1992), a biography *Phou Charong* (1995), a travelogue *Europagi Mapao* (2001), and critical essays *Wakma Maibi Amasung Atei Warising* (1999), *Haoreima Sambubi* (2000), *Amaibi: Manipurda Shamanism* (2006), and *Taungbo: Irawatki Aroiba Yahippham* (2015). She has also edited the anthologies *Manipuri Sahityada Nupigi Khonjen* (2003) published by Sahitya Akademi, New Delhi and *Loilam Matunggi Manipuri Seireng* (2017) published by Aseilup, Manipur. The recipient of many awards including the Sahitya Akademi Award in 2008 for *Idu Ningthou*, Memchoubi's poems have been translated into English, German, Italian and major Indian languages.

Dr Aruna Nahakpam (1959 -) is a writer, critic and educator based in Imphal, Manipur. The former head of the

Department of Manipuri Languages, Manipur University, her main publications are *Kunsuba Chahichagi Manipuri Upanyaas Neinaba* (1991), which discusses the Manipuri novel of the 20th Century and *Nongthangleima Amasung Taibang* (2001), a set of critical essays on aspects of Manipuri literature. Besides these, she has contributed essays and written forewords and introductions for various books published in Manipur. She currently serves as the president of Leimarol Khorjeikol (Leikol), the women writers' organisation of Manipur.

Ayung Tampakleima Raikhan (1942 -) is a writer, veteran sportsperson and social worker based in Imphal. She has also served as an announcer and programme executive at All India Radio (AIR) Imphal. She writes primarily in Tangkhul and has published a poetry collection *Avaram* (2011) and a short story collection *Mirinpam* (2015). She is the recipient of the Dr BR Ambedkar Samat Puruskar (2010) given by the Samata Sahitya Academy and the Panthoibi Awards 2010 given by Panthoibi Cultural Research Centre for Performing Arts, Manipur.

Bimabati Thiyam Ongbi (1960 -) is a writer and educator. Based in Imphal, she teaches in a government higher secondary school in Manipur. She has three published works to her credit: two short story collections *Khongchat* (1992) and *Etheikhraba Echel* (Short Story, 2014), besides a collection of essays on the norms and etiquettes within the royal palace of Manipur entitled *Manipurigi Ningthoukon Amasung Chatna Lonchat* (1996).

Binodini, the single name that M.K. Binodini Devi (1922–2011) wrote under, was a Manipuri novelist, writer of short stories and essays, playwright, screenwriter, and lyricist. Her collection of short stories *Nunggairakta Chandramukhi* (1965) was the first by a Manipuri woman. She was also the first woman recipient of the Sahitya Akademi award from Manipur which she won in 1979 with her historical novel, *Bor Saheb Ongbi Sanatombi* (1976). Some of her other works include the radio play *Ashangba Nongjabi* (1967), a translation *Amasung Indrajit* (1990), a travelogue *Ho Mexico* (2004) and a memoir *Churachand Maharajgi Imung* (2008). She also wrote a number of lyrics, besides scripts for award-winning feature films, ballets and documentary films including the internationally renowned films *Imagi Ningthem* and *Ishanou*.

Chongtham (o) Subadani (1955 -) teaches Manipuri Language and Literature at Standard College in Imphal. She has published three poetry books: *Pari Nangbu Kanano* (2002), *Diwaligi Meira Pareng* (2009) and *Sinthari Pirang Atom Bomb na* (2018). Two of her books – *Pari Nangbu Kanano* and *Diwaligi Meira Pareng* – have been translated into English. A columnist and freelance writer, her writings are also regularly published in local newspapers.

Dr Chongtham Jamini Devi (1936 -) is an educationist and prolific writer with more than 20 publications in Manipuri, English and Hindi languages to her credit. This includes five travelogues, four short story collections, two poetry collections, two memoirs, five prose works and four essays. Among her writings are the travelogues – *Swargagi Leibaktuda* (1994), *Korouhanbana Ironnungdagi Khongdoirakpa Lamduda* (1998), *Kohinoorgi Masaigonda* (2001), *Akashi Gangagi Torbanda* (2009) and *Surdhuni Gangagi Mapanda* (2013); short story

198

collections *Combing Operation* (1996), *Loinaidraba Wari* (1990), *Nungshi Khudol* (2006) and *Chekladugi Aroiba Bidai* (2010); poetry collections *Leinam Chandrabasu Leirang Satli* (2008) and *Taro Warise Shinaigang* (2013); and memoirs *Gangagi Matambakta* (2005) and *Tirtha Yatrik* (2013). Formerly the first Chairperson of the Manipur State Commission for Women, among her many awards are the Manipuri Sahitya Parishad's Sahitya Bhusan (2012) and the Dr BR Ambedkar Award (2010).

Guru Aribam Ghanapriya Devi (1965 -) is a lawyer by training, a dance artiste by profession and a writer by choice. Presently working as senior staff artiste at the Regional Outreach Bureau, Ministry of Information and Broadcasting, India, in Imphal, her debut short story collection *Thamoigee Liching* (2001) won the Dr Mayengbam Kamala Sheirol Mana in 2018. Her second book, a drama, *Nungshi Khonggul Liba* is in press at present.

Haobam Satyabati Khundrakpam ongbi (1953 -) is a teacher and writer. Her published works include the short story collections – *Mallaba Dairy* (1976), *Poknapham* (1995), *Eigi Nupagi Macha* (2005) and *Rai* (2012), novel *Sakhangdabi* (1984), and narrative poem, *Mainu Bora Nungshi Seirol* (2018). She has also written radio plays among which her works *Emagi Sana Matum* (1980), *Hingu Amasung Hinghallu* (1988) and *Hingbagi Mahao* (1999) have been broadcast on All India Radio (AIR), Imphal. She is also a recipient of the Khaidem Pramodini Gold Medal for her book *Eigi Nupagi Macha* in 2007.

Dr Haobijam Prema Chanu (1981 -) has written two poetry collections – *Angangba Eeshing* (2007), *Punshi Khongchatsida*

(2011) and a book of critical essays *Manipuri Sheirengda Ayibishinggi Khonjel* (2014). She teaches Manipuri Literature at Modern College, Imphal.

Dr Koijam Santibala (1960 -) is a poet, critic, actor and educator, currently teaching Manipuri Language and Literature at the Manipuri Department in Manipur University. She has six published works to her credit – the poetry collections *Amuba Meetkhumphee* (2004) and *Pallon Wangma* (2013), children's play *Tal Taret* (2006), monograph *Thoibi Devi* (2010), and critical essays *Theatre Amadi Sahityagi Wareng Khara* (2006) and *Manipuri Sheirengda Nationalism Amasung Atei Wareng Khara* (2013). She is a recipient of many awards including the Sahitya Akademi's Bal Sahitya Puruskar (2010) for her book *Tal Taret* and the Maisnam Oja Tombi Critic Award (2018) given by the Manipur Sahitya Parishad, Imphal.

Kshetrimayum Subadani (1959 -) works as a Child Development Project Officer (CDPO) in the Manipur Government's Social Welfare Department. Her published works includes the poetry collections *Mangkhraba Eesheigee Sur* (1975) and *Pigee Wari* (1995); novel *Laibak* (1982); short story collections *Nahakpu Eigee Kanano* (1978), *Nungee Chinbal* (1987), *Yeningthana Lakpada* (2000) and *Meisha Amasung Meichak* (2012); and biographical stories *Shaknaiba Kharagee Wari* (2008). She has also produced a number of publications for children including folk tales *Prithibigee Phunga Wari Khara* (1994), *Bharatki Phunga Wari Khara* (1998) and *Awang Nongpokki Phunga Wari Khara* (2002); a children's book *Prajatantra Chatpa Leibak Amagee Wari* (2001), and a comic *Illustrated Folk Tales of Manipur* (2010). Among the many awards she has received are the Dr Ambedkar Fellowship Award (2000), Best Award For Children's Literature (2001), Rabindranath Thakur National Award (2014), Hijam Irawat National Award (2015) and Sahitya Bhushan (2015).

Kundo Yumnam (1983 -) is an artist based in Manipur. She works with paintings, drawings, installations, etc. and is interested in the grey areas that overlap between the personal and the political. Her work has been exhibited/featured at World of Wearable Art, New Zealand; Exhibit320, New Delhi; and Religare Art, New Delhi. She was a resident artist at Peers 2011 organised by KHOJ, Delhi; and TheWhyNotPlace 2011 organised by Religare Arts. Aside from practicing art, Kundo is involved in activism for informed choices in healthcare and human rights in childbirth. She is also interested in exploring food in the context of health, social and cultural significance.

Dr Lairenlakpam Ibemhal (1958 -) is a poet and educator, currently teaching at a government higher secondary school in Manipur. She has two collections of poetry to her credit – *Leiron Chankhraba Thajaba* (1993) and *Nongthang Gee Innaphee* (2002). Her second work, *Nongthang Gee Innaphee* won her the Dr Khoirom Tomchou Memorial Gold Medal awarded by the Manipuri Sahitya Parishad, Bishnupur Branch in 2003.

Moirangthem Borkanya (1958 -) is a poet, novelist and short story writer. She has written four novels *Singareigi Leikada* (1993), *Leikangla* (2006) and *Nakenthagi Yenning* (2011); a novella *Meitei* (2003); six poetry collections *Loinaidraba Thawaigi Eeshei* (1988), *Utol Amadi Uchekshing* (1991), *Shangbannaba Atiyagi Ipakta* (1995), *Yeningtha Nangna Khongdoi Hullakpasida* (2008) and *Henjunaha* (2018); and a short story collection *Ningtambagi Mamal* (2007). She won the Sahitya Akademi Award in 2010 and also the Manipur State Award for Literature in the same year. Her other awards include the Khaidem Pramodini Gold Medal (1998), the Manipur State Kala Academy Award (2005), the Telem Abir Cash award (2008) and the Tayenjam Jayanta Poetry Award (2010).

Mufidun Nesha (1963 -) is one of the first women writers from amongst the Muslim community in Manipur. She has published two poetry collections – *Aroiba Khonjel* (2001) and *Mingshel Da Leichil* (2006). Based in Imphal East district, she is presently employed as a Supervisor in the Manipur Government's Social Welfare Department.

Natalie Nk (1988 -) is a young poet based in Imphal, Manipur. She writes primarily in English. Her poetry has appeared in *Brown Critique* (2012) and *Eclectica Magazine* (2013). She regularly reads poetry at open mic sessions organised by 'Kekru', an arts and literature initiative in Imphal.

Nee Devi (1968 -) works as Hindi Consultant at the Jawaharlal Nehru Manipur Dance Academy, Imphal. She has six published works to her credit including two novels *Kadaidano* (1987) and *Cheithengpham* (1988), a poetry collection *Chakngai Warisida* (1995), as well as two short story collections *Shollaba Mari* (2001) and *Lei Mana Amatang* (2009). She is the recipient of many awards including the Khaidem Pramodini Gold Medal (2004), the Katha Creative Award (2005) and the Manipur State Kala Akademi Literary Award (2014). An approved lyricist for All India Radio (AIR), Imphal, she has dramatized many of her own literary works as well as works by other renowned writers including MK Binodini's 'Nunggairakta Chandramukhi' and Elangbam Dinamani's 'Chhuti Chhuti Kalen Chhuti'. Three of her short stories – 'Namat Mangba', 'Khongbu Chadraba Khongloi' and 'Chakthung' have been made into films by renowned award winning directors.

Dr Nepram Maya Devi (1960 -) teaches Manipuri Literature at Pravabati College, Manipur. She has three publications to her credit: two short story collections *Wakat* (2004) and *Ngangleinaba Ethak Epom* (2010), as well as a travelogue, *Leikanglaga Shak-Khangnaba* (2006). She is the recipient of many awards including the Manipur State Kala Akademi Award for Literature – Creative (2015), the Khaidem Pramodini Sanagi Medal (2011), the Khoirom Tomchou Sanagi Medal (2013), and the Jamini Sunder Guha Gold Medal (2014).

Ningombam Sunita (1965 -) is a writer and teacher based in Thoubal district, Manipur. She has published two short story collections – *Khongji Makhol* (1997) and *Akaiba Mingshel* (2004). She received the Khaidem Pramodini Gold Medal Award (2001) and the Sahitya Akademi Award (2001) for her debut publication *Khongji Makhol*.

Ningombam Surma (1973 -) is a writer and teacher based in Thoubal district, Manipur. Her published works are the short story collections *Paokhumna Hangli* (2001) and *Ithak Machasinggi Wahang* (2007) – the latter won her the Ningombam Pramodini Ningsing Sahitya Mana (2009) award. She teaches at the Kakching Khunou College in Kakching district of Manipur.

RK Sanahanbi (Likkhombi) Chanu (1962 -) is a teacher, lyricist and writer. She has 12 published works to her credit – three poetry collections *Phijol Honglasi Ima* (2010) *Pibiro Ima Natambak Ama* (2015) and *Lan Khamlle Ima na* (2018); three lyrical poems *Sheihekki Hidenda* (2011), *Sheihekki Ipomda* (2013) and *Mellei Charronggum Ningthibi* (2016); three biographies *Esheigi Taibangda* (2011), *Matam Eesheigi Sheirengbasing* (2012), *Esheigi Taibangda, Vol.II* (2013); one short story collection *Thoklakkhini Thajadi* (2014) and a children's radio play *Thawaishinggi Thawai* (2017). She is also recipient of the Dr BR Ambedkar Fellowship National Award (2010), the Manipuri Sahitya Parishad, Meghalaya's Kabya Bhushan (2016) and the Khuraijam Phullo Sanathoi Mana (2017).

Sanatombi Ningombam (1964 -) is a writer based in Thoubal district, Manipur. She has published three short story collections – *Cactus Manbi* (1999), *Nahong* (2006) and *Ukugi Yumna Ngaihouri* (2013). She has received many awards. In her capacity as a teacher. These include, the Yambem Mani Sahitya Mana (2007), Priyosakhi Ningshing Sahitya Mana (2008), Chumthang Sahitya Mana (2013), Akoijam Chouton Rajkumari Muktasana Manipuri Sahitya Mana (2015) and Nameirakpam Chandreswar Ningshing Mana (2017).

Sanjembam Bhanumati Devi (1948–2018) is a writer, lyricist and translator. Among her published works are five poetry collections – *Khonjelsibu Nanggira* (1982), *Kallaba Eerei Amada Asum Asum* (1991), *Aroiba Wahang* (2001), *Laklo Eikhoi Pullasi* (2006), *Oiragadra Aroiba* (2011). She also translated Ruskin Bond's *A Flight of Pigeons* into Manipuri as *Khunusinggi Lanjen* (2004) for which she won the Sahitya Akademi Award for

Translation in 2007. She is also the recipient the Manipur Sahitya Akademi's Kavyabushan Award (2017), which was awarded to her posthumously.

Satyabati Ningombam (1960 -) is a writer based in Thoubal, Manipur. Recipient of the Thongam Udhop Literary Award, Dr Jamini Literary Award and the Chandrasakhi Chumthang Sahitya Mana. She has published six books – two poetry collections *Sana Apaibi* (1996) and *Itihaas Ki Eeshei Sakpi Ashangbi Ching* (1999), a children's book *Khunnou Laiphamgi Thouna Phabi Manishang* (1999), and three short story collections *Amangba Nonglakki Nongthang* (2000), *Nupi Amasung Mamising* (2007) and *Khunggangi Pukhri* (2010). She is currently employed as a Child Development Project Officer (CDPO) in the Manipur Government's Social Welfare Department.

Tonjam Sarojini Chanu (1960 -) is a writer and educator based in Manipur. Currently working as headmistress at a private school, she loves reading and gardening. The collection of poems, *Lan Khammu Ima* (2006) is her debut publication. She is also the recipient of the Dr Ambedkar Fellowship Award in 2006.

Yuimi Vashum (1990 -) is a freelance writer based out of Ukhrul, Manipur. She has a Master's degree in Journalism and Mass Communication, and an Honours degree in English Literature. She is currently guest faculty at North-East Christian University, Nagaland for Mass Communication. *Love. Lust. And Loyalty* is a collection of poem authored by her. Her writings can be found at yuimivashum.com.

Notes on Translators

Akoijam Sunita (1978 -) is an independent journalist and filmmaker. She has received many international and state awards for her writings on women, children, conflict, human rights and health issues. Starting out as a filmmaker in 2011, her first independent film *A Right To Dream* was produced by YourWorldView, a sister organization of the Commonwealth Broadcasting Association. She is based in Delhi and Manipur.

Bobo Khuraijam (1977 -), also known as Senate Khuraijam, is an independent filmmaker and journalist. Former resident editor for Manipur's leading newspaper in English *Imphal Free Press*, he is currently part of the Editorial Collective of *Yendai*, an online literary journal. His second directional venture, the documentary film *Ima Sabitri* was the opening film of Indian Panorama Section at the 47th International Film Festival of India (2016). Since then the film has won many national and international awards, including the Best Documentary Award at the 10th State Film Award (2016), the Silver Conch award for best documentary film (2018), the Satyajit Ray Golden award for best documentary film (2018), and the Best

Documentary film at the 4th International Film Festival of Shimla (2018).

Kundo Yumnam (1983 -) is an artist based in Manipur. She works with paintings, drawings, installations, and so on, and is interested in the grey areas that overlap between the personal and the political. Her work has been exhibited/featured at World of Wearable Art, New Zealand; Exhibit320, New Delhi; and Religare Art, New Delhi. She was a resident artist at Peers 2011 organised by KHOJ, Delhi; and TheWhyNotPlace 2011 organised by Religare Arts. Aside from practising art, Kundo is involved in activism for informed choices in healthcare and human rights in childbirth. She is also interested in exploring food in the context of health, social and cultural significance.

L. Somi Roy is a film and media curator, author, translator and publisher. He has curated film exhibitions across the world, including for the Asia Society, Museum of Modern Art, Lincoln Center and Smithsonian Museum. Founder and Managing Trustee of Imasi: The Maharaj Kumari Binodini Devi Foundation, he has not only published books by his mother MK Binodini, but also translated many of her works from Manipuri to English. Notable among his translations are the screenplay of the internationally renowned and award winning film *My Son, My Precious* (1981), Binodini's play *Crimson Rainclouds* (2012), and her memoir essays *The Maharaja's Household* (2015) and *The Girls' Hostel* (2016). Somi Roy is a conservationist and sports enthusiast working for the preservation of the endangered Manipuri pony and the promotion of international polo in India.

Natasha Elangbam (1977-) teaches in the Mass Communication Department at Manipur University. She enjoys providing narration for documentary films and has won the Rajat Kamal for Best Narration for the non-feature film *Sanakeithel* in 2008 at the 56th National Film Awards. She also writes scripts for documentary films and provides English narration for documentaries.

Paonam Thoibi (1983 -) is a clinical psychologist by profession and loves art too. Deeply engaged in conversations with people to know what goes in one's mind, she provides consultancy services to individuals and NGOs related to mental wellbeing and psychosocial activities. She also observes art likewise, to understand people and connect.

Sapam Sweetie (1992 -) is a poet and translator based in Imphal. She, along with her husband, organises 'Kekru', an initiative that thrives on poetry and its interaction with other art forms. Currently, they host open mic poetry sessions and publish chapbooks.

Shreema Ningombam (1984 -) is currently working as an Assistant Professor in the Department of Political Science, Nambol L. Sanoi College. Her poetry has been published in an anthology named *Tattooed With Taboos* (2015). She is pursuing her research in the areas of gender and sexuality in Meitei Society.

Soibam Haripriya (1982 -) is Fellow at the Indian Institute of Advanced Study (IIAS), Shimla. Her poems have appeared in anthologies and journals including *Tattooed with Taboos* (2015),

Samyukta: A Journal of Gender and Culture (July 2015), *40 under 40: An Anthology of Post-Globalisation Poetry: Poetrywala* (2016), *Guftugu* (July 2016), *Indian Cultural Forum* (June & September 2016). Most recently her poetry was part of *Centrepiece: Women's Writings from the Northeast* (2017), published by Zubaan and *A Map Called Home: Kitaab* (2018). Her present work examines the use of poetry in social anthropology, especially in the context of writing of ethnography in sites of violence.

Sonia Wahengbam (1977 -) started her professional journey as a journalist, working with *The Indian Express*, New Delhi, for almost six years as a senior sub-editor. Presently an Assistant Professor, she teaches Foundations of Print Journalism, Media Writing and Visual Communication at the Department of Mass Communication, Manipur University. She is also working on her PhD thesis 'Social Development through Traditional Media (Sumang Leela), with Special Reference to Manipur.' This is her first translation venture.

Thingnam Anjulika Samom (1973 -) is an independent journalist, writer and translator based in Imphal, Manipur. Her journalistic writing focusing on gender, conflict and developmental issues in Manipur has been published in many online and print publications in India as well as outside the country. She is the recipient of the Laadli Media Award for Gender Sensitivity 2010–11 (Eastern Region). She also translates literary works from Manipuri to English and was given the Katha Award for Translation in 2004. A few of her poems are part of the anthology *Centrepiece* (2017) published by Zubaan.

Glossary

AFSPA	Armed Forces Special Powers Act (AFSPA) 1958.
Ahaiyo! Tash!	Exclamation
Chigonglei	Fragrant acacia also known as the mimosa bush plant.
Chinghi	A herbal decoction of rice wash water and herbs used to wash the hair.
Hiyangei	Festival celebrated on the second day of the Meitei lunar month of Hiyangei (October-November) wherein daughters are given a grand feast and gifts in their parental home.
Imaipemma	Exclamation expressing great relief or disbelief, according to usage.
Indomcha	Aunt
Ine (also Iche, Ichemma, Ichebemma, Inemhal, Inemton)	Aunt, elder sister, elder aunt, younger aunt, all forms of address which are also often used in deference to age and social position.
Iromba	Spicy dish made by mashing boiled assorted vegetables with fermented fish and chilli.
Ita	Endearment term meaning 'Dear friend' used by one girl/woman to another girl/woman.
Iteima	Sister-in-law
Kambong	A type of aquatic edible plant

Kanglei	Meitei
Khudei	Loincloth used by Meitei males
Khwangchet	Cloth tied around the waist, like a sash, over the *phanek* or *khudei*
Kokshet	Headcloth, used by women and tied in a specific way
Kumlang	A type of black thread
Kwa	Betel nut. Also refers to the preparation of betel nut wrapped in betel leaves along with assorted condiments and meant to be eaten.
Kwa-manbi	A medicinal plant
Loukhao phurit	A shirt, worn while working in the fields.
Mey	Exclamation used, especially by kids expressing disagreement or defiance.
Mora	Low cane stool
Ningol Chakkouba	Festival celebrated on the second day of the Meitei lunar month of Hiyangei (October–November in the Georgian calendar) wherein daughters are given a grand feast and gifts in their parental house.
Nonggoubi	The greater coucal or crow pheasant (*Centropussinensis*) who, in Manipuri creation myths, did not take part in the dredging of the rivers as it was looking after its babies and household work. As punishment, it was not allowed to drink water from the rivers, lakes, and so on, and could quench its thirst only when rain fell.
Meira Paibi	The Meira Paibi ('torch-bearing women') movement of Manipur is a women's social campaign that started as a prohibitionist exercise against alcohol and evolved as a crusade to protect human rights against the atrocities of the armed forces during the counter-insurgency movements in the state.

211

Nupi Lan	Literally, Women's War', this refers to the two major movements spearheaded by women in Manipur. The first Nupi Lan was in 1904, when the Manipuri women rose against the imperial British order commanding Manipuri men to bring teak wood from Kabaw Valley and rebuild the burnt house of a British officer. The second Nupi Lan in 1939 was an uprising of the women to stop the export of locally produced rice out of Manipur – something that had created an artificial famine in the state. In both instances, they emerged victorious.
Phanek	Sarong-like cloth used as lower body garment by girls and women.
Phi	An upper wrap used by women.
Phumdi	Small floating island-like bodies on Loktak Lake, composed of aquatic vegetation naturally matted together with organic debris and soil.
Phunga	Secondary fireplace in the kitchen.
Singgarei	Coral Jasmine plant
Thaballei	Night Jasmine plant
Zarda	Chewing tobacco used in paan or betel nut preparations.